PRAISE FOR

breathless

"Once the central dilemma is set in motion, it becomes impossible not to hurry toward the haunting final pages."

—*Booklist*

"McDaniel's fans, who seemingly read with tissues in hand, will snatch it off the shelves." —*Kirkus Reviews*

"A heartstrings-tugging read." —*School Library Journal*

You'll want to read these inspiring titles by

Lurlene McDaniel

Angels in Pink
Kathleen's Story • Raina's Story • Holly's Story

One Last Wish Novels
Mourning Song • A Time to Die
Mother, Help Me Live • Someone Dies, Someone Lives
Sixteen and Dying • Let Him Live
The Legacy: Making Wishes Come True • Please Don't Die
She Died Too Young • All the Days of Her Life
A Season for Goodbye • Reach for Tomorrow

Omnibus Editions
Always and Forever • The Angels Trilogy
As Long As We Both Shall Live • Journey of Hope
One Last Wish: Three Novels
The End of Forever • True Love: Three Novels

Other Fiction
Heart to Heart • Prey • Hit and Run
Briana's Gift • Letting Go of Lisa
The Time Capsule • Garden of Angels
A Rose for Melinda • Telling Christina Goodbye
How Do I Love Thee: Three Stories
Till Death Do Us Part
Now I Lay Me Down to Sleep • To Live Again
Angel of Mercy • Angel of Hope
Starry, Starry Night: Three Holiday Stories
The Girl Death Left Behind
Angels Watching Over Me
Lifted Up by Angels • Until Angels Close My Eyes
I'll Be Seeing You • Saving Jessica
Don't Die, My Love • Too Young to Die
Goodbye Doesn't Mean Forever
Somewhere Between Life and Death • Time to Let Go
When Happily Ever After Ends
Baby Alicia Is Dying

From every ending comes a new beginning. . . .

Lurlene McDaniel

breathless

DELACORTE PRESS

Copyright © 2009 by Lurlene McDaniel

Scripture quotations marked (NIV) are from the Holy Bible, New International Version. Copyright © 1973, 1978, 1984 by International Bible Society. Used by permission of Zondervan Bible Publishers.

Visit us on the Web! www.randomhouse.com/teens
Educators and librarians, for a variety of teaching tools,
visit us at www.randomhouse.com/teachers

The Library of Congress has cataloged the hardcover edition of this work as follows:
McDaniel, Lurlene.   Breathless / by Lurlene McDaniel.   p.   cm.
Summary: A high school diving champion develops bone cancer in this story told from the points of view of the diver, his best friend, his sister, and his girlfriend.
ISBN 978-0-385-73459-2 (trade) — ISBN 978-0-385-90458-2
(lib. bdg.) — ISBN 978-0-375-89097-0 (e-book)
[1. Cancer—Fiction. 2. Assisted suicide—Fiction. 3. Friendship—Fiction.
4. Brothers and sisters—Fiction.]   I. Title.
PZ7.M4784172Bp 2009   [Fic]—dc22   2008018427

ISBN 978-0-440-24016-7 (tr. pbk.)

Printed in the United States of America
10 9 8 7 6 5 4 3 2 1
First Trade Paperback Edition

Abimelech went to the tower and stormed it. But as he approached the entrance to the tower to set it on fire, a woman dropped an upper millstone on his head and cracked his skull. Hurriedly he called to his armor-bearer, "Draw your sword and kill me, so that they can't say, 'A woman killed him.'" So his servant ran him through, and he died.

JUDGES 9:52–54 (NIV)

The fighting grew fierce around Saul, and when the archers overtook him, they wounded him critically.

Saul said to his armor-bearer, "Draw your sword and run me through."

But his armor-bearer was terrified, and would not do it; so Saul took his sword and fell on it.

1 SAMUEL 31:3–4 (NIV)

Dear Reader,

This is a book I've wanted to write for a long time, well over ten years. What intrigues me about the subject of euthanasia is the ethical dilemma it poses. I know, however, that a novel is built on characters and plot, and until recently the characters hadn't come together in my head. The plot hadn't jelled in my heart. Finally it did and I wrote *Breathless*.

What excited me then and still does now is the difference between ethics and morality. Some people explain that ethics are what we *say* we believe and morality is how we *act* on what we believe. We might say one thing, but when no one's looking, what do we do? In *Breathless,* my characters face this quandary and make difficult choices. Ultimately we all make choices in life, both good and bad. These decisions shape our character and create our life paths. Most choices do not involve life and death. The choices in *Breathless* do.

I hope you will give this novel about euthanasia serious thought. I'm still pondering the topic myself. Maybe you will ask yourself, "What would I do if this happened to me?" Maybe not. I certainly hope you never face such difficulties, but may this novel open your mind and your heart.

Best wishes always,

You don't know me yet, but please read this before you begin.

Most people believe they have a clear idea of what's right and wrong. Many say they know how they'll act, or how they'll handle an extreme situation. But to be honest, no one knows. Not really. Even if you say, "I'll never do this or that!" it actually might not be true. Because none of us truly knows what we'll do when the circumstances become so overwhelming and complex that we can't even tell right from wrong. And then there are the totally unforeseen situations, when life deals cards you never expected, or when something that's considered wrong morphs into something right and your mind determines that what once was the rule is not written in stone. Even if this has never happened to you, I'll bet you understand exactly what I'm talking about.

This is what happened to me. I thought I had standards. I believed in my absolutes. I did for most situations. Then I didn't. As time went on, my world turned gray and my absolutes became murky. Right and wrong dissolved into what I knew I had to do.

Please don't judge me until you hear my story.

COOPER

Travis Morrison became my friend in third grade after two fifth graders beat me up on the school playground. They said I was ugly and weird-looking, took my lunch, and made me cry. Travis shared his lunch with me, and after school when his mom picked him up, he asked me to play at his house. I went home with him every day after that. It's not as if my mom cared where I hung. She was working two shifts at the carpet mill. She said she was glad I was being cared for by a family with a mama who was a professional nurse, since I was prone to trouble.

Travis's family is normal—which mine isn't—and he has a sister, Emily, two years younger than he is. I think she's pretty, and I made the mistake of saying so one time. "Pretty?" Travis made a face. "Is your brain fried?" It took me a while to figure out that he really likes her but just won't show it. I have no sisters, and Travis is the closest thing to a brother I'll ever know.

I've never looked like any of the other kids at school. My dad was some Hawaiian guy who skipped out before I was born. I've seen photos of him. Mom's part Korean, so I admit I'm weird-looking by southern Alabama standards. Cooper Kulani: misfit. That's me.

By the time I was in seventh grade, I was a head taller than every other kid in my class. I could kick the crap out of any of them, and no one has ever shoved me around again. Except Emily. All she has to do is look at me and I turn to mush. No one's ever caught on, though. Not even Travis, who knows me inside and out.

Travis must have been born with the "risk-taking" gene medical science talks about. There isn't anything he won't do, or try to do. I guess that's why he became such a good diver. He has no fear and no equal in competitions. He's on track for athletic scholarships all over the country. I joined the team when he did but never liked it, which is why I never medaled, and one reason I quit the team last year. But for the most part, I do what Travis does, not because I have the risk gene, but because I was born crazy, I live hard, and he's my best friend. There isn't anything I won't do for him.

Emily

It isn't easy being the sister of the most popular non-football-playing athlete in the state of Alabama. Don't get me wrong. I'm not jealous of all the attention Travis gets. It's just a fact of life—I get lost in his shadow. I learned early on that girls wanted to be my friend to get to Travis, so I decided not to hang with most of them. Who wants to be used? I love to read, so books are my main friends. They're always available, always friendly, and always interesting, and they never make me choose sides.

Mom's a nurse, and she likes working the night shift best, which means she's home in the mornings when Travis and I get ready for school. She fixes breakfast, gets us all out the door, catches some sleep after we leave, is gone to work by four in the afternoon when we get home from school. Dad's an accountant and takes over dinner duty. He's our chauffeur, cheerleader, homework guru, and sometimes room mother. He's a much better cook than Mom anyway.

I like school. I make good grades; I like rules. No guessing what to do or how to act. God has rules. My parents have rules. Schools and governments and society and Internet sites, they all have rules.

My brother, of course, has never met a rule he could obey. He makes life up as he goes along, and if I ask him why he does something, he smiles and says, "Why not?"

Travis is a champion diver. Dad calls him "focused." I think he's a fanatic about his sport. He spends a ton of time practicing and competing, and didn't even have a serious girlfriend until last year, when he hooked up with Darla Gibson. She's one of the highest-profile girls at Robert E. Lee High, though not necessarily in a good way. She doesn't have the best reputation, but that doesn't bother Travis. To me she seems fluffy, like a jar of marshmallow creme or a wad of cotton candy. Pretty to look at, not very deep, will make you sick if you get too much of her. I can't figure why Travis likes her—except for the obvious—but he really likes her.

Then there's Cooper, Travis's lifelong friend. He has an after-school job nowadays, but he used to hang at our house all the time. He has straight black hair, eyes so dark they look black, and a snake tattoo wound around his upper right arm. I've never heard him talk about his family and can't remember ever meeting them. There must be a reason, but I can't figure it out, so I let it go. Haven't seen or heard anything in school either, but Cooper keeps to himself. I guess everyone has secrets. Even me! True confession: He makes my insides go hot and squiggly when he comes around, but I'll never let him or Travis know.

Cooper, Travis, and Darla will be juniors in the fall, and I'll be a freshman, which means that they'll graduate in another year and I'll be left alone, the kid sister who stands outside the spotlight that shines on her brother.

When we went to the lake on the first day of summer vacation, I thought everything was great. It never occurred to me that real life has no set rules.

Darla

"Tits for brains." That's how my father talks to me. It's how he puts me down. And his words hurt sometimes as bad as his fist. Sure, I didn't get a ton of gray matter at birth—he's a member of that Mensa society and thinks he's too smart for the real world. And maybe I didn't get showered with his "smart" DNA, but I don't see why he has to throw that in my face all the time. His mean mouth made my sister Celia leave home the minute she graduated. I'll be out of here soon as I graduate too. He's not so mean to Kayla. She's ten and already showing some of Dad's brilliance, which makes her more acceptable. Celia and I never were smart enough.

As if he's made something of himself. Mom's

got the job and brings home the paycheck. Dad sits in his home office and writes books that don't sell—which of course is the fault of "stupid editors who can't recognize real talent."

I want to be an actress—Darla Gibson, star. Sure, lots of girls say that. They want the fame and fortune, want to see themselves on the big screen with people falling down worshiping them. Nice perks, but I want more than that. I want my work respected. The acting bug bit me in first grade when my teacher cast me as a tomato in a little play she wrote about healthy eating. Mom came to watch me, but Dad couldn't be bothered. He said, "A tomato? It's because you're fat." I cried about that one.

I've learned to tune him out. Mostly. Lately he says I've gotten "lippy," and that gets me slapped more often, but better that he hits me than Mom. He wails on her sometimes.

In middle school, I went kind of wild and got a reputation that followed me to high school, where I met Travis. Miraculously, he's the first guy who likes me for me and not because of my body. A girl knows when a guy's using her. I've had enough experience with that kind of boy. But

Travis isn't that way. We talk about everything. Sometimes all we do is sit and hold hands and talk. I love Travis with all my heart.

He tells me I'll be a great actress too. I tell him he'll medal in the Olympics someday. We believe in each other. Our lives are perfect when we're together. I had no clue our lives would change until the day at the lake.

Travis

I should have been born a fish. For me, H_2O is the perfect compound. When I was little I might have been the only kid on the planet who liked to take baths! But it's underwater where I feel most at home. The world is quiet in the deep, cool water; a little mysterious. Aquaman is my favorite superhero because he can breathe underwater. I used to think, Wow. If I had gills, I'd never come up.

But I'm not a competitive swimmer. I'm a diver. People don't understand that swimmers and divers are different kinds of people. Swimmers like the surface of water. Divers like going deep.

The springboard used to be my specialty. In high school meets, athletes can only compete on the springboard. In club and college competition, it's different. The first time I climbed onto the ten-meter platform, I knew I'd found my place in the sport. And I'm good at it. College coaches are calling me from Florida, California, and even the Ivy League schools. They all want to talk to the boy who "leaps fearlessly while executing dazzling tucks, twists, pikes, and somersaults before his ripped entry," according to a local reporter. I have to admit, the guy got it right. (Humility is overrated.) I practice for hours to be the best.

So on the first day of summer vacation, me; my friend Cooper; my girl, Darla; and my kid sister, Emily, head out to Alabama's Lake Martin, where we can cruise around the small islands in Dad's boat with its bad-ass oversized outboard motor.

I cut the motor as we near Chimney Rock, the tallest and most awesome of the natural island cliffs. The water is a hundred and fifty feet deep at its base. I aim the nose of the boat at the pebble beach nearest the rock.

"What are you doing?" Emily asks. "I thought we were going to ski and have a picnic."

"And we are. What's wrong with eating here?"

She looks up at Chimney Rock. Darla and Cooper follow her line of sight.

"Tell me you're not going up there to jump," Coop says.

"I'm not jumping." I leap into waist-high water and drag the boat by its anchor rope toward the empty beach.

Emily says, "Travis . . . ," in her "I'm warning you" voice.

"I'm going to dive."

Darla squeals.

"You are not," Emily shouts. "Kids have died jumping off that rock!" She looks at Cooper. "Stop him."

"When have I ever been able to stop your brother from doing anything?"

"Dad will kill you!" Emily says. Her face is all panic-stricken.

"If the fall doesn't," Coop adds.

"Who'll tell him?" I ask.

Darla scrambles over the side and grabs my arm. "Are you sure, Travis? It's a long way down."

"That's why I'm leaving you three here on the beach with the food while I make the climb." I look at Emily. "You can close your eyes."

Emily crosses her arms and shoots daggers at me with her eyes.

"Divers do this all the time off the cliffs in Mexico. Even higher," I remind her. "And besides, I've done it before."

"When?"

"Last summer. Just me and Coop."

Cooper throws up his hands. "I just watched."

"You two are so stupid!" Emily shouts. I laugh, but her words cut Cooper. I think he likes my sister. The doofus.

By now, our boat is beached and the others are scrambling onto the shore. Cooper swings the cooler onto dry land. Darla looks worried, but she trusts me. I kiss her. "It'll be all right. The hard part is the climb. The trip down is over in a flash. Just save me some food."

I take off toward the back side of the cliff, knowing I've got a steep climb. But I'm pumped. I'm sweating by the time I get to the top, and my right leg hurts. It's hurt a lot lately, but I ignore it like I always do. Coach Davis doesn't like hearing his athletes piss and moan.

I limp to the edge, where I wave to my watchers below. They look pretty small from so high up.

On top of the great rock, I stare toward the horizon where the lake meets the sky, and I watch boats buzzing around looking like windup toys.

The day is perfect, hot and clear. All sun and sky and blue water. My heart is racing, and something like an electrical current is rushing through me. I plan my strategy for the dive, decide not to get fancy. I'll execute the pike position once, hit the water vertical and clean.

I jump, and I hear my leg bone crack before I feel the pain that follows me all the way down into the deep, dark water.

Emily

We hear Travis scream the minute he bobs up in the lake. He thrashes and I think he's drowning. Cooper hits the water at a dead run, swims like a torpedo out to where Travis is floundering, and grabs him under the arms. My brain kicks in and I run after him. Darla and I meet them halfway to the beach, but Cooper shoos us away. "Let me get him on shore."

"No," Travis says through clenched teeth. "My leg. I can't stand. It hurts. Oh man, it hurts."

"Get the boat," Cooper says, and Darla and I scramble backward, grab the hull, and push it away from the island toward the deeper water.

Cooper gets a kickboard under Travis's leg for support and uses rope that he cuts from the anchor line to secure it. We keep Travis afloat while he works.

Darla can't stop crying. I'm crying too, and when I find my voice, I ask, "What happened? Did you hit something? A rock?"

"Don't know." Travis's words are moans. "Happened when I jumped. My thigh."

I can see a hump under his skin near his hip, where the skin is turning dark purple, and I feel queasy. "Looks broken. There's some aspirin—"

"Not a fix, little sister." He's pale as milk.

I'm shivering and shaking and Darla's scrambled into the boat to help, but she's clueless and keeps begging Cooper to tell her what to do. We've left our cell phones in the car back at the marina, because they wouldn't have worked out here on the lake. Cooper says we can't leave Travis and go for help either. We need to get him into the boat and back to shore.

Cooper slides his arms beneath Travis's body in the water. He warns, "This is going to hurt." He tells me to get into the boat and for me and Darla to use our weight to pitch it as far to one side as we can without taking on water. We do, and the small boat dips sideways even with the deadweight motor. With amazing strength Cooper lifts Travis and the board out of the water and over the railing. Travis stifles a scream as the board slides inside and onto the bottom. Cooper shoves the boat farther out, leaps inside, and starts the motor.

Darla wedges her lap between Travis's head and the hard fiberglass floor of the boat, and while my brother cries with pain, we smash across the water toward the shore.

I call and tell Mom about the accident, and she says to meet her and Dad at the hospital ER. Cooper gets Travis on the backseat of Cooper's old car, and Darla sits on the floor by Travis's head. I jump into the front. Cooper breaks every speed limit getting Travis to the hospital.

Having a nurse for a mother is a huge benefit, and Travis moves quickly into triage with Mom and Dad. The rest of us are banished to the waiting room.

In the aftermath, I feel my knees wobble.

Cooper takes my arm to steady me. "You all right?"

"No."

He leads me to a chair. The room is cold and

our swimsuits are still damp. Fortunately, we had shirts in the car, or Darla would be standing around in her bikini and every eye in the place would be on her big boobs. I hug the shirt—an old one of my brother's—close to my skin, wishing I had something to cover my legs.

Darla asks, "Would you like a Coke? There's a machine down the hall. I'll go get you one. If you want one."

"A Coke's fine."

"What do you think happened?" Cooper asks.

I shake my head.

"And how long does it take before we know something?"

"I don't know." I look up, suddenly conscience-stricken. "We should pray."

"What?"

"We should pray and ask God to heal him."

Cooper's black eyes stare hard at me. He says, "Sorry, I don't believe in God."

I've never heard anyone say this out loud. When you grow up in the Deep South, belief in God is embedded in your DNA. We pray before football games, before school starts, when anything happens that's out of our control. Travis and

I have church enrollment cards from nursery school through high school. I still attend youth group and Sunday school, so Cooper's announcement shocks me. "But God's real," I say.

"Not for me."

Darla's back with my Coke. "What's wrong?"

"Emily wants to pray for Travis and I don't believe in God."

Darla says, "I believe in God."

"Well, good," Cooper says. "Then you two pray."

Before I can say a word, Cooper adds, "Wait. Here come your parents."

I throw myself into Mom's arms. "How is he?"

"His leg's broken—his femur—thigh bone, up high near his pelvis."

"Can they fix it?" This from Darla.

"They want to check him in."

"Can't they just set it and send him home?" I ask.

Dad says, "Can't set the bone until the swelling goes down."

Cautiously Mom says, "They want to run some tests."

"What kind of tests?"

"We can talk at home. Right now, we want to get him settled upstairs."

"What do you want us to do, Miz Morrison?" Cooper speaks up.

"Go home. Take Emily—"

"Please let me stay," I say quickly. "I—I want to see Travis."

"You're half naked," Mom reminds me.

Dad steps between us. "I'll run her home to change, then we'll come right back."

I don't want to leave, but Mom's making the rules.

"I want to see him too," Darla says, looking frightened.

"Tomorrow." Mom pats Darla's hand.

"We'll go take care of the boat," Cooper says.

For the first time I think about our boat, which we've abandoned on the shore near the marina. Our cooler is back at Chimney Rock too.

"I'd appreciate that," Dad says.

Cooper is halfway to the door when Darla bolts after him. "Wait for me!"

Once they're gone, Mom walks to the elevators.

"Let's go, honey." Dad puts his arm around my shoulders.

A hundred questions are banging around inside my head. I ask none of them. Whatever happened to Travis is more than a broken bone. I've been the child of a nurse too long to not know better.

Travis

"You could have drowned." Mom tells me that one too many times.

"But I didn't." After three days trapped in this hospital bed with nothing but medical tests and daytime TV game shows and soap operas for entertainment, drowning doesn't sound all that bad. "When will they finish with me? I don't want to spend all summer in the hospital."

Mom crosses her arms. "Not until Dr. Madison figures it out."

"They've taken a gallon of blood. What's with that? Just tell him to set my leg and send me home."

"He has the medical degree, not you," Mom says.

I've had accidents before—stitches, a concussion, a broken arm once when I was five—and I was never checked into the hospital. "That doesn't mean the guy knows what he's doing."

Mom's mouth makes a straight line that tells me to back off. I grumble, "If I'm stuck here, I need some decent food. I'm starving."

"I get you double helpings." She leans down, kisses my cheek. "I've got to go on duty. Your dad and Emily will be here shortly."

"Can they bring some ice cream?"

She doesn't answer. I pick up the TV remote and surf for old *Star Trek* episodes. Beam me up, Scotty.

Once we're alone in my room that afternoon, Emily chews me out about my dive. Her hair's pulled back in a ponytail, her face is sunburned. "It was totally stupid!" She looks about twelve, with an angry grown-up expression, but I let her vent.

"Hey . . . it's a broken leg. It'll heal."

"And you'll jump again."

"Probably."

"That's not funny."

I take her hand. "Look, sis, we are who we are.

You're a thinker, and you figure all the angles before you do something. Not me. I like the adrenaline high, and that's never going to change."

She grumbles, "I would have figured out I'd get hurt if I jumped from the top of Chimney Rock."

"It never crossed my mind," I tell her honestly.

"It should have. You're not Superman."

"You've never flown. You don't know how it feels." I yawn. I'm getting sleepy because of the drugs they're giving me.

"Should I leave?" she asks. Her anger's gone and she looks worried.

"Your call. Can't be much fun to hear me snore."

"I'll wait." She settles in a nearby chair and doesn't let go of my hand.

It's late at night when Cooper comes to my room. "Hey, man."

I'm awake but groggy. "Don't let the nurses catch you. It's after visiting hours."

He taps his closed fist against mine. "I didn't want to run into the paparazzi."

I grunt. "Dad's running interference. Just a few reporters checking in so far."

"Yeah, I saw it on the news. Big story, along with Mrs. Ford's dog tearing up the flower beds at City Hall."

I grin. Alexander's a small place, and because so many alumni are still around, high school athletics has a big following. Football is king, but my honors in diving have given me supporters. "Not the way I want to be remembered," I say. "For a failed dive."

"What's that?" Cooper points to a machine by my bed.

"Happy juice." I hold up a button linked by a tube to the machine that runs into a vein on my arm. "A morphine drip. I push this, and I'm happy."

Cooper nods. "Don't go liking it too much."

"Never happen. The stuff makes me loopy. It clogs my brain."

Cooper doesn't crack a smile or give a comeback.

I take a deep breath. "Thanks for saving my butt."

"Would have ruined the picnic if you drowned."

Better, I think, more like the old Coop. He's always got my back.

"You get the boat to the house?"

"Yeah. Hosed it down and cleaned it up."

"I freaked all of you out, didn't I?"

"Did you freak yourself out?"

"A little," I admit. "When I couldn't swim, couldn't kick . . . no control. I hate not having control."

"That's why we need the buddy system," he says. "Don't do that again."

I grin up at him. "You sound like Emily."

He looks away when I mention my sister. "They going to let you out of here anytime soon?"

"Don't know. I have an MRI tomorrow. A kind of whole-body X-ray," I explain.

"I'll see you tomorrow night. You can tell me if they discover a functioning brain."

I don't want him to leave. "Until then," I say, and flick the button on my morphine drip. "Just me and my happy juice."

He grins. He's the best guy on earth and majorly underappreciated by most people at school. He acts tough and scary, but because of where he lives, it pays to have creeps afraid of you. I've always kept his secrets, especially about his mom.

"Thanks, Coop." The morphine spreads through me, but he's already gone.

Darla comes to visit twice a day before she hits her summer job at the theater concession stand where she works five nights a week. "The money's shabby, but it gets me out of the house," she told me when she first took the job. "Plus, I have another mouth to feed."

"Your car." Her grandmother left her some money when she died, and Darla's mom helped her buy an old car. She works for gas money.

"And clothes," Darla added. "I need new clothes."

"What's wrong with wearing your bikini?"

She makes a face. "Goose bumps."

She's my babe. Plus, she's beautiful and smells like flowers and gives me a high that beats morphine by a mile. Most guys see her rack first, which I'll admit is impressive. I see her eyes. Big, blue, full of feeling. They look inside me and make me want to be better than I am.

"Things all right at home?" I understand about her wanting to be away from her house. Her old man's a real piece of work. I think he hits her; I know he hits her mom.

Her pretty smile droops a little. "I just stay out of his way."

Another reason to be out of this hospital. The two of us should be hanging at the lake or at my house to keep her away from the guy. "Soon as I'm out of here—"

She kisses me. "Just get better, Prince Charming."

I pull her into my hospital bed—strictly forbidden—and we heat up the sheets before a nurse can find us.

Between CT scans and MRIs and lab-tech blood-lettings, visitors start to hit my room. Coach Davis, my swim coach; guys from the team who aren't away on vacation; adults and kids from church; two pastors; mere acquaintances; friends of my parents; even a few more reporters pop in. Seeing Coach and the guys is the hardest, and it makes me miss my life even more. "The team needs you," Coach tells me, "so get better."

"Diving's my whole life. I'll be back."

He squeezes my shoulder. "It takes a bone around six weeks to knit. Plenty of time for you to heal and get back in the gym and rebuild the muscle before school starts."

Weight lifting is good conditioning, so Coach

requires his team to spend so many hours a week working out. "I'll be ready when school starts," I say.

"You're the best we have," he says seriously. "Probably the best in Alabama. Stay healthy."

My head swells with his praise. "I won't let you down, Coach. I swear."

Emily

"*I*t's osteosarcoma. Bone cancer."
Mom's words hit me like stones. I can't say a word.

"The tumor just starts growing. Boys are more likely to get it than girls because their bones grow so fast. Random error from DNA gone amok." Her voice cracks. "No way to predict who'll get it. It just happens."

We're at home in the family room on a sunny summer morning. Light floods through the windows, and the ceiling fan whaps the air with long blades. The smell of bacon from breakfast hangs in the air. She and Dad are on the sofa and I'm sitting cross-legged on the floor in front of them. A *House and Garden* picture of a perfect family. "But . . .

but Travis isn't sick." My feeble protest as the picture begins to shatter.

"The bone in his leg is sick."

"What are they going to do?"

"Chemo and radiation. And surgery."

"To cut out the tumor?"

"To cut off his leg."

I think I'm going to throw up. "But they can't!"

Dad's eyes are bloodshot and Mom's barely holding herself together. "They must."

"Does he know? Have you told him?"

"We're meeting his doctor at noon and we'll tell him together."

"Me too?"

"No. You're staying here."

"But . . ."

Mom drills me with a look. In truth, I don't want to be there. I don't want to see the light go out of my brother's eyes.

COOPER

Emily called crying and told me the news. Once we hung up, I went out on the cement pad in back of our trailer and began wailing on my punching bag. Sweat is pouring into my eyes. My arms are heavy and my knuckles sore inside the gloves. It doesn't matter. Nothing matters. The doctors are going to cut off Travis's leg.

A neighbor's dog is barking, and someone yells, "Shut up!" The dog yelps in pain and I slump to the ground and hang my head. I can't help the dog. I can't help Travis. I can't help Emily. I'm good for nothing.

I get up, turn on the hose, and take a long drink. I douse my head and neck to cool off. I go inside the trailer, where it's dark and the AC wall unit and two tabletop fans are barely keeping the place cool. The air stinks. Dishes are piled in the sink and the garbage can is overflowing. I should clean it up. If I don't, no one else will.

I'm hungry, and I glance at the clock. It's after two and I haven't had anything to eat since last night. My summer job at the burger joint starts tomorrow. Until then, I'm on my own. I hear Ma snoring in the back above the racket from the AC. I walk to the bedroom and crack open the door. She's lying half on, half off the rumpled bed. I go inside, scoop up her feet, and position her better on the bed. She grunts but doesn't wake. On the nightstand I see a half-empty vodka bottle. She hasn't worked in weeks, but she still manages to buy her booze.

"Get a job, Ma," I say quietly. My paycheck won't stretch far enough to cover rent and electricity, food, gas for my car, and her booze.

I wonder what other guys talk about with their mothers. Wouldn't they tell them about their best friend having cancer? Mine probably doesn't remember that I have a best friend.

I pull an old soiled comforter over her, see her purse on the floor and pick it up. Inside

I find a twenty-dollar bill. I know how she came by it.

I should go to the hospital. I can't. Not today. Travis needs time to think this out for himself.

I leave the bedroom, grab the keys to my old Pontiac off a wall hook, and head out to buy food.

Travis

"Liars." That's what I say when the doctors tell me. Mom is teary eyed and Dad's face is stone. Dr. Madison has come with another doctor, an oncologist, Dr. Wolfsen.

"I know this is a shock—"

"You're wrong," I say. "I can't have cancer. I feel fine."

"Your leg isn't fine," Dr. Madison says. "There's a tumor in the bone. That's why it broke."

Mom reaches out to touch me, but I jerk away.

"We'll start treatment at once," Wolfsen says.

"I don't want you to cut off my leg." I feel like I'm going to puke. If I do, I want it to get all over him.

"Chemo first," Wolfsen says, as if I haven't

spoken. "Then the surgery. Then more chemo. Radiation probably. We'll run more tests. Sometimes, if the cancer is localized, we can do a bone graft and save the limb. I don't expect that to be the case for you, though. I'm being honest with you, Travis. I'm always honest with my patients. I won't give you false hope."

"You can't cut off my leg!" I say it louder to make sure he hears me this time.

"And we don't want you to lose your leg, but if we don't amputate, and if the cancer spreads—"

"And it will spread unless we amputate," Dr. Madison says.

Wolfsen keeps looking at me. "—you will die."

Blunt. To the point. A leg for my life. They consider it a good trade-off. I'm not sure I do.

"There are prosthetics—" Mom starts.

I squash her words with a look. Fake legs. I've seen video clips of wounded soldiers with artificial limbs valiantly jogging while a reporter shoves a microphone in their faces and applauds their courage. I've watched the Wheelchair Olympics on TV. That's not who I want to be. No diver ever won medals with a missing body part.

"Go away," I say.

Before Mom can protest, Dad takes her arm. "Give him space."

All the space in the world won't make me feel better about what they want to do to me. Wolfsen says, "I'm starting a chemo infusion immediately. The first protocol will be short and intense. You'll be an outpatient. You'll have physical therapy and a physiologist who'll help you learn to use your prosthesis when the time comes. And you'll see a psychologist too. You'll get through this, Travis. You're young and strong, and if the cancer hasn't spread beyond the tumor, survival rates are sixty to eighty percent."

"And if it has?" He's trying not to scare me, but I stare him down.

"One thing at a time," he says.

"We'll fight it," Mom says.

"It's not your leg," I tell her.

"We'll get through this," Dad says quietly.

I hear their use of "we," but this is happening to me. To my body. To my life. To my future.

Cooper knows because Emily's told him. He looks ready to explode when he comes to visit.

"I keep looking at my leg, trying to imagine it gone," I tell him.

"How did you get cancer?"

"Don't know. I just did." I close my eyes. "I don't want them to cut off my leg."

Cooper shoves his fist into the mattress of my hospital bed. The blow is strong enough for me to feel vibrations. "It sucks."

I can't get my mind around never walking on my own two legs again. "You should have let me drown."

"Don't talk that way."

I take a deep breath. "Guess it'll be Lenny Feldman's time to shine." Feldman has been my main competition, chasing after the same medals as me. He's a good diver, but I've beaten him out for top honors at every meet. I tell Coop, "I'd been looking forward to kicking his butt at state. Guess he'll laugh his head off over this turn of events."

"No one will be laughing," Cooper says. "You made him a better diver by competing against him. Now he'll just be ordinary."

My throat clogs up when I think about not looking down on pool water again with judges and teammates watching. I want to feel the cool water on my skin so bad I can taste it. I want to plunge beneath shimmering water into the quiet world of blue silence. I feel my eyes get wet. I turn my head so Cooper won't see my weakness.

"You can still dive," he says. "You'll figure it out. I know you. You don't give up."

I search for a spark of determination inside me. I come up empty.

Seeing Darla, telling her, is hardest of all. My beautiful girlfriend. Blue eyes crying. I put my arms around her, knowing what I have to do. "It's okay, babe."

"But cancer," she says. "That's so awful. My grandma had cancer."

"That's what this is for." I hold up my arm with the IV line leading to the bag of chemicals on the stand next to the bed. I'm already feeling a little sick—they said I might—but the cancer diagnosis doesn't affect me like the leg amputation does.

Darla pulls away, fumbles for a tissue. "My nose is dripping."

"You're still pretty."

She laughs a little. "I love you."

"Yes. About that."

"What about it?"

"I'll understand if you . . . if you . . ." I can't get the words out.

"If I what?" She squints. "Are you dumping me?"

My arm burns where the chemo is going into my vein. "I'm telling you that you can move on. I'll understand."

She's perched on the bed and jumps off. "Is that what you want?"

"No. I—I just think you need to review your options."

"My options? Do you think I have a Plan B because you're sick?"

Nothing's coming out the way I thought it would. "A lot of guys will be interested in you if I'm not in the picture. If you want to—"

"Want to what?" she interrupts me. "Get a new boyfriend? One who doesn't have cancer?" She's looking angry.

"It's the leg too, Darla. No more of a lot of things we used to do together. You should have a choice."

She's glaring at me now. "I'm making my

choice. The leg thing doesn't bother me. So you'll have one leg. Big deal."

I get angry. "Well, it's big deal to me! No more diving. I'll have a piece of equipment strapped to my *stump*." I say the word with all the hatred for it that I feel. "I'm losing part of my body, Darla. They're cutting off my leg. Don't you know what that means?"

She drills me with her pretty eyes, leans forward, so close to my face I can see her pores. "Yes. I know what it means. It means you'll weigh less."

Her answer is swift, and it strikes me as funny. Not just funny, but hysterically funny. I laugh. I laugh until I ache, and she laughs with me. We laugh until we're crying. I pull her against me, and in that moment, I've never loved her more.

Emily

Travis's situation goes onto the prayer chain at church—that's when names are passed along to every person in our congregation for specific prayer. The pastor prays for him during regular Sunday service. The youth pastor prays for him during group time. My Sunday school class prays for him before starting lessons. I hear the words "I'm sorry" a hundred times from about as many people. Everybody's sorry about what's happening to Travis. I don't know what to say back. "I'm sorry too"? The words hardly fit because it's all so unfair.

I'm sad, but I'm angry too. God could fix this if he wanted. That's what God does—answers prayers and fixes people. I've been taught this all my life. Didn't we all pray for the Williams baby, born prematurely? And didn't the baby get better and come home, and isn't she healthy now? Does God love the baby more than Travis? And if he does, why? What did Travis do to make God mad at him?

Mom tells me, "Disease happens. It's random sometimes."

Dad says, "We need to keep our faith strong."

Travis asks, "Where's God when I need him?"

I'm confused and sick inside my heart.

I sit in church. I say, *"Kyrie eleison."* Lord have mercy. The plea to the Divine sounds more serious in Latin. *Kyrie eleison. Christe eleison. Kyrie eleison.* I repeat the words over and over.

I promise God I'll be good forever if he'll just make my brother well.

Darla

I sit alone in the dark theater after midnight. My favorite place to sit and think. A few of the films in the cineplex are still running; I hear sounds through the walls, the car chases, the final screams of a horror movie. But in this theater it smells like stale popcorn, and the screen is dark and silent. I remember my first date with Travis. We came to the movies. We held hands. That's all. My hand in his. No "accidental" brushing against me. No groping my leg or my boobs in the dark. Just his hand holding mine. Respect. I think that was the night I began to fall in love with him.

My friends couldn't believe he was Mr. Nice Guy. They'd expected him to be conceited and out for himself. I admit I expected him to be that way too when he first asked me out. But I was wrong. After Travis and I had been dating for a couple of months, Dad came out of his den long enough to look him over. Travis was polite, Dad suspicious. Later, at the dinner table, I decided to ask Dad what he thought of Travis. Dad said, "Guys are just out for what they can get off you."

"Travis hasn't asked me for anything."

"Like you're an expert? I was a teenage guy. I know what he wants. Just wait. He'll pounce."

"Ken, give her a break," Mom, the quiet one, broke in.

"Shut your mouth," Dad told her.

Mom looked down, pulled the napkin in her lap.

I was sickened by him, as usual, because he didn't need to yell at her. He broke her spirit long ago. I don't know why she stays.

He turned on me. "You'll end up like your sister."

I pushed away from the table. "Celia's plan was to get out of here," I told him.

"Some plan!" he fired back. "Now she's got a kid and a good-for-nothing freeloader living with her."

"I guess you know all about freeloading."

He jumped up and I was sure he'd take a swing at me, but I bolted up the stairs and locked myself in my room—Celia's old room—and I cried. I miss my sister. What happened to her won't happen to me. I'm smarter than that. And Travis isn't Fred.

The side door opens and the manager sticks his head inside the dimly lit theater. "That you, Darla?"

Mr. Cain. "I'm just sweeping up the place." After the concession stand closes, we're expected to clean the ten smaller theaters.

"You look like you're just loafing in the dark."

"Taking a breather."

"Could you hurry it up? Your shift ended almost an hour ago. I'm not paying overtime."

I stand. "Yes . . . sure. Someone stuck gum on the back of this seat."

He swears. "No respect for property anymore. What's the matter with you kids?"

He bangs out the door and I start scraping the gum off the chair. I used to look at movie screens and imagine myself on them. Darla Gibson, movie star. See me, Daddy? Do you see what I've become? A star! I pull off a wad of sticky gum and drop it into a plastic bag I use for cleanup duty. It all seems so silly now, this wanting to rub my father's nose in my success. Travis has cancer and is losing his leg. No star power can fix that.

He'll get a replacement leg. He's showed me pictures. It's made of titanium with a jointed knee and ankle and a beige shell-covering like that color in a box of crayons. And the leg has a naked mechanical foot that can wear any shoe—"matchy shoes," Travis says sarcastically. "How nice."

The pamphlet reads, "A technological marvel. Looks real to the eye." It doesn't look real. And it isn't flesh and blood. It isn't human. He's told me that he hates it.

Tears sting my eyes. I wish I'd yelled at Mr. Cain and told him that all kids aren't disrespectful and mindless of others' property. Some kids are great. They're nice, kind, thoughtful, talented, gifted, wonderful. And through no fault of their own, they still get cancer.

Travis

So now it's over and the surgeons have taken off. Funny way to think about it. "Taken off" has a double meaning: the cutters have gone, my leg is gone. Taken off. Get it? I sit in the hospital bed and stare down at my bandage-wrapped thigh. All that's left. A stump. "No," Mom insisted when I first used the word. "It's a residual limb."

"It's a stump," I say. "Call it what it is."

"It had a tumor," she says. "It was diseased and it would have killed you."

My stump hurts. I'm wigged out on morphine again because of the pain. Crazy, but I can still feel my toes. They said this would happen. Phantom pains. Mystery feelings in a leg no longer attached. My brain hasn't bridged the disconnect yet. No leg. No toes. No tumor. Be happy.

Where did they put it? What do they do with sawed-off legs? Did they bury it? Burn it? Give it to a medical school for doctors-in-training to cut and dissect? I guess it doesn't matter. Gone is gone.

I hear someone moving in my room. It's not a nurse, because one has already come and checked me and gone. A big shape materializes beside my bed. "Coop?"

"Yeah, man, it's me."

I'm groggy, not sleepy. "I thought you were the grim reaper."

"That's not funny."

"What time is it?"

"Midnight."

"I guess you heard."

"Emily and Darla both called me. I was working."

The pathology report came back this afternoon. The cancer was found in three lymph nodes—a bad sign.

"Now what?"

"More chemo. Radiation. Mom's got specialists lined up in Birmingham."

"I'm sorry, man." His voice is thick.

He straightens. I grab his wrist. "I don't want

them to keep cutting me up. I won't give up any more body parts."

"You're going to beat this thing. Whatever it takes."

I know he's right, but at the moment, I have no fight left in me. I know he needs to get home and catch some sleep, but I don't want to be alone. "Can you hang awhile?"

He eases down into a chair. "As long as you want."

Emily

Dad's outfitted the house to make life easier for Travis. The den downstairs is now a temporary bedroom until he gets strong enough to climb the stairs. The bathroom shower stall has grab bars. Dad's ripped out carpeting and put down new flooring, and there are no more little rugs around the house. Nothing slippery. Everything's about Travis now.

His car is parked on the grass beside the driveway. I've kept it washed and cleaned, and I start the engine every day to make sure it runs. Dad's fixed up our front sidewalk because a crack in cement can cause Travis to have a bad fall. I've taken over lawn duty while my brother's recovering and learning to walk on his new leg.

The day Travis comes home, I hang a "Welcome Home" banner across the front door and string balloons over the door to the den. Cooper and Darla are waiting with me. She's baked cupcakes—kind of pathetic-looking little lumps smeared with frosting that's oozing off the top and down the sides in the heat, but I don't think anyone notices except me.

When Dad pulls into the driveway, he and Mom hop out and slide open the side van door. "Phil, get the wheelchair."

"No," Travis says. He picks up crutches from beside him on the seat.

"Please, honey. Let's be safe."

He gives Mom a wilting look. "I want to walk into the house."

Dad offers his arm for support, but Travis ignores him.

Cooper, Darla, and I stand on the porch and watch Travis slowly maneuver up the walk. My brother's lost a ton of weight and his skin is sallow-looking from the chemo. His empty pants leg is pinned up so that he won't trip on it. Darla grips my elbow, and Cooper slides his arm around my shoulders. We all hold our breath.

At the bottom of the porch steps, Travis looks up at us and asks, "How would you score me?"

It takes a second for his question to sink in.

"Ten," I say. "A perfect ten."

Once we get Travis settled in, I corner Darla and Cooper before they can leave. "We need to help him."

"How?" Cooper asks.

"He shouldn't spend too much time alone. His shrink says he's depressed."

"Go figure."

"I'll do anything to help," Darla says.

"What do you have in mind?" Cooper wants to know.

"Make sure he has plenty to do all summer. Games, DVDs—just hanging out with him between chemo and physical therapy. If we're around him, if he's not alone thinking about what's gone, it'll make him feel better. That's what Mom says. Positive attitude, you know."

Without a second's hesitation, Darla says, "I can be here most days. Until I have to go to work."

"I'm good for the night shift," Cooper says.

"And I live here," I say. "I'm available anytime."

This makes Cooper laugh and I blush. Why do I feel like a little kid whenever I'm around him? "Okay, then. We have a plan," I say, sounding like a social director. Awkwardly I hold out my fist the way I've seen Travis and Cooper do. Guy code. The three of us tap our fists together, sealing our pact.

COOPER

The last time I cried, I was eleven. Watching my best friend struggle up his front porch with a missing leg is one of the hardest things I've ever done. I want to seize him around the middle and haul him up. But of course, I can't.

Once we are all inside the house, he drops the crutches, leans on me, and hops to the sofa. "Crutches bite," he says. He's sweating from the exertion.

Darla scoops up her plate of cupcakes and presents them to Travis. "Hope you like chocolate and white icing."

"You bake these, babe?"

"In my Easy-Bake Oven," she jokes.

He pops one into his mouth. "Yummy."

She blushes, and I get that they're not talking about cupcakes.

Travis looks around. "My new digs?"

"Just until you can get up the stairs," Mr. Morrison says.

"Yeah, just until I get your room repainted bubble-gum pink," Emily says.

He pokes at her with his crutch. "Watch it, Em. My arms are five feet long these days."

"Just until you get situated," his mom says.

Darla snuggles next to Travis on the sofa. They look cozy, like they always look together. The crutches could be a prop if you don't notice the gap on the floor where Travis's foot ought to be. And no one's even mentioning the elephant in the room—the cancer that's still inside him. I say, "I need to split. I'll be back tomorrow after my shift ends."

Back home, I pound on my punching bag until my arms ache. And I cry like a girl.

Travis

Mom picks me up from outpatient, where I've had chemo dripped through the shunt in my chest for an hour. I go to chemo twice a week and get hooked up to IV bags, and the port in my chest takes the poison slowly into my body, where it hunts for cancer cells to destroy. Trouble is, it's destroying other cells too. The chemicals they're giving me are so strong that if they leak onto my skin, I'll need plastic surgery to repair the damage. The poison sucks my energy. In mirrors I look wasted, like a meth addict, but chemo is no recreational drug.

I hunch down in the car, pick up a plastic bowl, and hold it under my chin.

Mom glances at me sideways. "Do you feel sick?"

"A little." The stuff they give me includes anti-nausea meds. Sometimes they help. Sometimes they don't. Today they don't.

"How's the other going?"

I'm working with a physiotherapist on parallel bars. I've been practicing just standing up and putting weight on what's left of my leg. Pain shoots through me until I see stars. The stump of my thigh has to toughen up. My therapist tells me it sometimes takes months to master walking, but I'm determined to do it a whole lot quicker. The first time I held the leg, I couldn't believe it would hold me up. It's hinged to do the work of a leg, with a silicone liner that has to be turned inside out and washed every day. I wear a tubelike sock over my stump, and it has to be kept clean too or I'll develop nasty sores. Care and maintenance is lifelong. I'm bionic boy now.

"The skin's sore. Walking's harder than I thought it would be." I answer Mom's question.

"When you were a baby, you didn't crawl," she says. "You just pulled yourself up on the coffee table and started to walk. Couldn't be bothered with that intermediate process of crawling."

"Maybe I should crawl now."

"You'd hate it as much now as you did then." She reaches over and squeezes my arm.

"Things would go faster if it weren't for the chemo."

"I know, but we've got to kill the cancer."

This protocol is worse than the first and is scheduled to be a whole lot longer. I'm anemic and I've had a kidney infection, which has set me back. I feel dizzy now, and nauseated. "Better pull over," I say to Mom. "I'm not going to make it home."

She pulls off on the shoulder of the road and I open the car door and heave. Mom's around the side of the car in a flash, holding my head and wiping me clean with towels she keeps in the back-seat. When I'm finished, I fall against the seat. "Sorry."

"No problem."

"Did I get any on you?"

"Occupational hazard."

I'm grateful Mom was with me. Cooper could handle it, but I don't want him to have to. School starts soon, but I won't be returning. "I can't go back to school like this," I tell Mom after she's cleaned me up.

"I have a tutor lined up. Return whenever you're ready."

I wonder if I'll ever be ready.

I know what Emily, Darla, and Cooper are doing. They think I don't notice how they're always showing up, never letting me be alone, always making sure Travis is covered. When I get home from treatments, Darla's usually there, and all I can do is stretch out on the sofa and fall asleep. When I wake, my head's in her lap and she's reading a magazine. "You don't have to stay," I tell her.

"There's no place else I'd rather be."

I want to believe her, so I do.

After she leaves, Cooper usually shows up. When he does, Mom invites him for dinner and he wolfs it down. I'll bet it's the only good meal he has every day.

The best days are when we all go out to the lake. Sometimes we take the boat out, but most of the time we stay on the shore, off by ourselves, just me and Darla, Cooper and Emily. Being around the water makes me feel good but sad too. I've been told I'll swim again, and maybe I will. But I'll never dive again, at least not for medals.

Sometimes I dream about diving, about feeling the water on my skin as I knife through the surface. I'm happy in the dream, and I can breathe underwater. And then I wake up. When I wake, the den is lit only by a nightlight and someone's covered me with an afghan. Mom's handiwork. Make sure the one-legged boy can find his way to the bathroom in the dark. Make sure the one-legged boy doesn't get cold at night. Make sure the one-legged boy has friends who look out for him, who stand ready to make sure he's busy and not alone.

They all mean well. But they can't know how the dark space inside me is growing. I lie to them. I lie to the shrink. I can't get out of the dark hole. "Peace is here," it whispers.

Darla

I'm in front of the trophy cases at school getting teary-eyed. The cases take up the greater part of a wall and are filled with memorabilia that goes back to the 1970s.

I see old faded football and basketball jerseys, medals, trophies, and photos of former star graduates and district- and state-winning teams. The last glass case is the newest, and is a mini-monument to Travis. He's perhaps our greatest athlete in ten years, a diver headed for sports immortality. Photos of him grin out at me; medals hang from his neck in a glittering array, like jewelry, like stars that will now go out because their sun no longer burns.

I sniff and hug my stack of books close to my

chest, suddenly aware of a group of boys at the other end of the case. One says to me, "Want me to hold those for you, Darla?"

I whip my head in their direction as the others in the group snicker, and see Bud Tucker, quarterback for this year's football team and a former boyfriend. "Drop dead," I say.

"Hey, no way to talk to an old friend."

"You're no friend of mine," I say.

He comes closer, the group moving with him like a pack of jackals. "We were good friends once upon a time."

He's the main reason my rep is bad. I had sex with him in eighth grade and he spread it all over middle school. He told me he loved me, and like an idiot, I believed him. He told everyone else I was easy but worth the takedown. "Once upon a time is over," I say.

"I hear your main man is down for the count."

"Don't talk about Travis."

"I feel for him. We all do. But that doesn't mean you should be alone. I'll take you back."

He moves in so close to me I can feel his breath. He makes my skin crawl. Then I say the wrong thing. "You're not worthy to tie his shoes."

Bud pounces on it. "There's only one shoe to tie now."

His friends think it's funny and laugh like crazy. If looks could kill, they'd all be lying on the floor. I stare him down. "Get over yourself, Bud. And don't make me compare body parts with your friends standing around. Next to Travis, you come up short in that category by a mile."

Before he can recover, I stalk off. I round a corner and run smack into Emily. She gives me the once-over.

"What were you talking about with Bud Tucker?"

"Nothing worth repeating."

She stares hard. "Are you going to dump Travis for Bud?"

I'm so shocked that I can't speak.

"Are you?"

Hot tears sting my eyes. "How can you ask that? I love Travis. I spent the whole summer with him because I love him. I won't leave him."

She breaks eye contact. "Okay," she mumbles.

It hits me that she doesn't really like me. I'm not sure why. "I won't bail on Travis. That's not the kind of person I am."

"Will you come over like you did in the summer?"

I know a lot of responsibility has fallen on Emily's shoulders. Her parents expect her to hustle home so that Travis won't be alone between the time their mother goes to work and their dad comes home. "I'll be there every day. Trust me, no one will miss me at my house."

She gives me a funny look but doesn't press the issue. "I—I would like some time to do things after school. It's hard when I have to go straight home."

"Problem solved," I say cheerfully.

"I won't be busy every day. Just once in a while."

"No need to explain," I tell her. "Travis is stuck with me. And so are you."

I spend as much time as I can with Travis. His tutor comes in the mornings, but the afternoons are ours. I do homework at his house, go home at the last possible minute. When he feels good, we ignore the homework. In his room, we're in our own private world. I sit on the floor with my books spread out and he lounges on his bed with his books.

One afternoon I catch him staring at me. "What's wrong? Is my face on crooked?"

He grins. "I think you're beautiful."

"And I think you're sweet to say so."

He's raised up on his side, wearing long flannel pajama bottoms that hide his missing leg. "Why are you on the floor when I'm up here?"

"Can't think of a good reason." I stand, climb onto the bed, and lie beside him. I snuggle into his bare chest. "You feel good," I tell him.

"You smell good," he says, playing with my hair.

"New shampoo."

"Buy stock in the company."

He scoots closer until our bodies are molded against each other and I can feel him through the fabric. I stroke his side, run my fingers under the band of his pj's. I hear his breath catch. I love him so much. I wasted myself on Bud Tucker. Travis is worth a hundred of guys like Bud. "How long will we be alone?" I ask.

He looks at the clock on his bedside table. "Maybe another hour."

"Good. Then we've got time."

"For?" His voice is soft in my ear and his breath warm against my cheek.

"For whatever happens," I say. I rise up, pull my shirt over my head.

He gazes at me, touches my skin lightly. I see in his eyes how much he wants me. "Are you sure?" he asks.

Goose bumps make me shiver. I lower my mouth to his. "Way sure," I tell him.

Travis

There's a woman in chemo with me, Sally, a single mom with bone cancer after having had breast cancer. We come on the same days and end up in side-by-side reclining chairs for our drip sessions. "How you doing today?" she always asks. "Isn't it a beautiful day?"

It doesn't matter what the day's like. Sally always says it's beautiful. "It's pouring rain," I tell her.

"Don't matter. So long as we're alive, it's a beautiful day." She's toothpick thin, and she wears a turban because the treatments have made her bald. Her eyes close and I watch her take deep breaths. Finally her face relaxes. "Yoga," she says. "Transcendent state. You could try it."

"I'll stick to morphine."

Her two little girls, five and seven, sit and color in a corner, watching TV and acting like this is the most ordinary thing in the world, that everybody's mother gets hooked up to chemo. "I signed a DNR today," she tells me.

"What's that?"

"If I code—die—then I don't want them to bring me back or hook me up to life support."

"You can do that?" New information for me.

"I don't want to be kept alive if I can't get well. I don't want doctors sticking feeding tubes and breathing tubes into me. And I surely don't want my girls to see me turn into some kind of vegetable they have to take care of all their lives. And they'll have lives because their grandma will finish raising them. It's all arranged."

"I didn't know you can decide for yourself."

Sally nods. "Adults do. Kids your age, well, parents decide."

I look at her girls coloring happily. "What about if it was one of your kids?"

"Oh, now, don't go backing me into a corner."

"But, what *if*, you know, what if the doctors wanted one of your girls to go on life support?"

She watches them for a few moments. "Would depend on what kind of life she would live after she came off life support. Being in pain like I am changes you and the way you think. No use hanging around God's good earth if you're a burden to anyone."

For the rest of the afternoon, all I thought about was what would my mother do if it happened to me?

I'm at home, downstairs in the family room at two in the morning, when I hear rapping on a window. It takes me a minute to find my crutches and hobble over. I look out and see Cooper. I raise the window and cold air slaps me in the face. "What're you doing out there?"

"I need a place to crash."

He stinks of beer. "You okay?"

"Open the door. I can't get through this window."

I make my way to the front door and he lurches inside, almost knocks me over, but catches himself with the wall. I steady him with a crutch. "What's going on?"

His eyes are glassy. "The old lady's entertaining. Nowhere else to go."

I get it. He's crashed here before when he can't go home. "Come in, but be quiet."

He's in his shirtsleeves. "Too cold to sit in my car all night. I saw your lights were on."

"It's all right, man. You can have the sofa."

He makes it there and drops to the cushions. "What are you doing up, anyway?"

"Can't sleep. My days and nights are all turned around."

"Sorry." He rests his forehead in his hands. "I feel like crap."

"You drunk?"

"Not drunk enough."

"I can make some coffee."

"No. I want to crash." He stretches out and pulls our old quilt over himself. "You sure this is okay?"

"I said it was." I lower myself into Dad's recliner.

"Your mom won't freak when she finds me here?"

"She's never freaked before."

"Good mom," Cooper says, his voice slurry and thick.

I'm sorry Cooper doesn't have a mom like mine. I guess it's better that I'm the one with cancer and not him. I push back in the recliner and let Cooper's instant snoring lull me to sleep.

Emily

I bounce into the family room Saturday morning and stop dead in my tracks. Cooper's asleep on our sofa, Grandma's old quilt pulled to his waist. His arm is shielding his eyes. Asleep, he looks like a little boy. My heart trips, and I want to touch him.

"Don't poke the sleeping bear," Travis says. He's come up behind me on his crutches.

"Why is he here?"

"Got locked out."

I know he's covering for Cooper, because the smell of stale beer hangs in the room. "You better air out the place before Mom and Dad get up."

"Mom's still asleep, but Dad's in the kitchen

flipping pancakes. Open the window. I'll wake him."

I do as I'm told, ignoring Cooper's groans while Travis rouses him. Cooper lets go with a stream of swearing, sees me, and stops abruptly. "I've heard worse," I say over my shoulder.

Travis snorts. "In the movies."

I shoot him a nasty look.

"My bad," Cooper says.

Dad comes into the room with a steaming mug of coffee. "Here you go." He hands it to Cooper, smiling cheerfully. "I know how you feel. I tied one or two on myself when I was in college."

Cooper groans.

"Want a cup, Em?"

"A cola for me."

"You should get something in your stomach," Dad tells Cooper. Minutes later he returns with a plate of griddle cakes in one hand, a cola and a bottle of syrup in the other. "Eat up."

Travis follows Dad out of the room. I don't know whether to go or stay. I finally decide to stay, and sit on the other side of the coffee table on the floor, facing Cooper and feeling self-conscious.

Cooper soaks the pancakes with syrup. I

watch, fascinated, while he cuts the stack with his fork and shovels it into his mouth. "Want some?"

"I'm a cereal person," I say.

He grins. "Twigs and grass. Yummy."

I hug my knees. I can't recall a time I've ever been alone with him.

His dark eyes connect with mine and I go hot all over. Cooper leans back without breaking the connection. His dark eyes roam my face and my body. He grins and hands me his plate. "Think your dad has more food ready, little sister?"

I scramble to my feet, breaking the spell he has on me. "Go ask him yourself. And I'm not your sister or your servant."

His laugh chases me out of the room.

Later I'm in the laundry room sorting dirty clothes with Mom when she says, "Can I ask you something, Em?"

"Sure." I heave a bundle onto the floor.

"Are you attracted to Cooper?"

My face flames and I stand stock-still. "Mom! I've known him forever."

"That's not an answer." She leans against the washer. "I'm not prying."

"Sounds like you are." I feel squirmy.

"It's a logical question," Mom says. "And it wouldn't surprise me. He's familiar. He's always hanging around—"

"Because of Travis."

"Partly. I—I just don't think he's the best choice for you."

"You're the one who took him in when he was a kid." I turn defensive.

"He needed our family at the time, and it was the right thing to do. But I don't want you falling for him. He has . . . problems."

An understatement, I think. Cooper's a loner, nobody's friend except Travis's. "I don't think that's going to happen." I turn so she won't see the lie. I am attracted to Cooper. I think he's exotic and sexy. "He hangs with a different kind of girl," I tell her. The girls he chooses don't have great reputations, and he never stays with any of them for very long.

I sort dirty clothes silently until Mom says, "Look, I know it's been difficult for you with all the attention going to Travis, what with him being so sick. I'm sorry, but that's the way things are right now. I need to know that I don't have to worry about you, Emily. That you won't divide my loyalties."

"You don't want me to have a boyfriend. And you really don't want it to be Cooper. I get it, Mom."

She offers an apologetic smile. "You've always been smart, so maybe that is what I am saying. It won't always be this way."

I resist the urge to argue.

"When Travis was two, I found him on top of the bookshelves in the living room. On top! He'd climbed up there while I was changing your diaper. He's always been on the edge of life, and now he's really on the edge."

"He didn't ask to get cancer."

"That's not the point. It's just that now he's the focus of our family. He has to be. It doesn't mean we love you less. If anything, I'll depend on you more."

That's me, Emily the Dependable One. Her trust feels like a wool coat in summer. I bend down and pull the light-colored clothes away from the dark ones and put them into a separate pile. "I know how to be good, Mom," I say.

"You are good, Emily, and this won't go on forever with your brother."

And then it will be your turn. That's what she's telling me. That's what she means. What I don't say is that I'm not even sure how to take my turn.

COOPER

Travis returns to school in January. He walks in to a hero's welcome, a ceremony in the gym with most of the school attending. The jocks sit in a big group—Coach's idea, to show how much he's been missed. I can tell Travis doesn't want this kind of attention. People are staring at his legs. He's wearing jeans, but the athletic shoe on his prosthetic foot looks new and way too clean.

Coach makes a speech. Then the whole swim team surrounds Travis, and a photographer from the local paper snaps some pictures. Travis looks like he wants to bolt. Finally it's over, and kids file out to classes. I bulldoze my way through the crowd to my friend.

"Get me out of here," he says under his breath.

"I'm taking him home," I tell the principal. She looks baffled, as if she can't understand why Travis doesn't want to bask in the glow of the celebration.

Darla and Emily circle Travis. "I need to go home," he tells the principal.

"We'll take him," Emily says.

"All three of you?"

"We'll be back before third period," I say.

She agrees, and we cut to the door.

Outside, the sun is bright, the day cold for southern Alabama, and I feel like we've been let out of jail.

"Did any of you know they were going to do that?" Travis asks. We shake our heads. "Because if I'd known, I'd never have come back."

"They wanted to honor you," Emily says.

"For what? I haven't done anything except survive and relearn how to walk. A three-year-old can do as much."

We pile into my car. "Where to?" I ask.

"The lake," Travis says. "I don't care if it's cold. I want to be near the water."

"What about coming back by third period?" Emily asks.

"Get a grip, sis," Travis says. "We're not coming back today."

"We'll do the drive-thru and get fries," Darla says. "Warm us up." She finds a blanket and tosses it over herself and Travis.

I look over at Emily in my front passenger seat. Her face is beet red. I tell her, "I can bring you back if you want to come."

"I don't want to."

I'm betting she's never cut a class in her life. "Still playing by the rules, huh," I tease her, and her face gets even redder.

"I'm not a kid," she growls. "Stop treating me like one."

If I treated her the way I want to, if I took her in my arms . . . I put the brakes on my train of thought and drive to the lake.

Darla

Life's been rocky at my house. Dad's temper is hair-trigger; he explodes over the smallest things. No need to burden Travis with my problems, so I keep mum, but this is how I'll remember my senior year—my dad yelling and slamming doors and my boyfriend sick with cancer.

My father had a meltdown last night and actually slapped Mom. After it happened I raced upstairs and held my pillow over my head. I feel bad about retreating, but I wanted to stay out of his way.

Later I find Mom in the kitchen, pressing an ice bag to her face. I'm sorry for her, but I'm angry too. I say, "You shouldn't let him get away with hitting you."

"You're right. He's not good at controlling himself. He didn't mean it. He said he was sorry."

"Don't defend him, Mom."

"He's had a bad month and he's frustrated."

"Well, if he ever does it again, you should take Kayla and leave. Or call someone to help you deal with it. You shouldn't let him get away with excuses."

She dismisses me with a hand wave. "Oh, Darla, I won't leave. You know that."

"But it's not right. It's against the law."

"This is our home." She hardly listens to me. "I know he shouldn't have done it, and I know he's sorry. I love him. And he loves me. I know he does"

I want to shake her. I know what love is, and it isn't about yelling and not at all about hitting. "I'm getting away from here right after high school, and you know that," I tell Mom. "You and Kayla should come with me."

"Marriages have their ups and downs. One slap isn't right, but it also isn't grounds for leaving, Darla. You're young, and you don't understand how people can get angry at one another but still love each other. My life isn't yours."

She's right—I don't get it. Dad's losing control more often, and she acts blind, or worse, just lets it go. "Well, if he ever looks like he's going to hit you again when I'm in the room, I'm going to get in his face. I won't stand around while he smacks you. You should tell him to stop."

"It won't happen again," she insists, trying to soothe me. She shifts the ice pack. "He truly loves me—all of us. He's just so very unhappy right now. He's suffering."

I don't say, "He's mean and rude and always has been," like I want to. I tell her, "I think you should leave if it ever does happen again. Don't let him get away with that."

She studies me with eyes that look old. "And what about Travis? Will you walk just because he's sick and you're tired of watching him suffer?"

"I'll never leave him." I bristle at the idea. "Don't even compare these things. I love him."

"Then you understand perfectly how it is for me. So don't get all uppity and tell me what to do, Darla. I'm not leaving your father."

"It isn't the same at all!" I say. "Travis didn't ask for cancer."

But she isn't listening. She walks out of the kitchen, leaving me to sit alone in the dark feeling furious at the unfairness of life. Travis is good and kind and sick, and my father is healthy and mean and unworthy of my mother's love.

Travis

A diver understands statistics.

Two summers, my junior and half of my senior years, since they took my leg.

Five months of remission.

One relapse.

Second remissions are harder to achieve. Third remissions are almost impossible. I know the odds. I'm keeping score. Zero hope.

This is how I think about my life: Before I got sick, endless possibilities. After? No possibilities.

I started my senior year full of determination. Now I've stopped going to school altogether. The principal says that I can graduate if I finish my work at home. Fine. Suits me. It's hard hanging around the classroom when I feel rotten, even harder when I see kids horsing around and I haven't got enough energy to stand up. I miss diving. It's like an ache in my gut, the wanting to be up there on the board. Our team lost the district title my junior year. Everybody says we'd be state champs if I were still on the team. They'll get another shot at it in a couple of months, but I never will again. It's over for Travis Morrison.

Everyone expects me to be strong and courageous. Mom and Dad see me as a fighter. Cooper thinks I'm invincible. Darla sees me as brave. Emily believes I'll triumph and get well.

The other afternoon, when Darla was with me, I understood how cut off I am from my old life. She was happy, all excited, telling me all about her upcoming tryouts for the senior play and how she was going to win the lead from all comers.

"Mrs. Paulson hasn't told us what the play will be. We're just supposed to show up in the auditorium, and that's when she'll give us the book for a cold reading. Can you imagine? So impromptu—wonder what play she's picked? Anyway I can't wait. I'm good at impromptu."

I used to be excited about the future too,

pumped before every competition, eager to talk to every recruiter who called or wrote. Once, I was going to be a great diver. I saw myself as fearless, a champion, ready to take on the world. Once upon a time.

Emily

*F*or a brief few months, Travis went into remission, and we thought he was on his way
to full recovery. Hope was smashed five months
later, just after the start of his senior year, when
cancer was discovered in his lungs. He went back
into chemo, and then into dialysis because his
kidneys are failing due to the chemo. A vicious
cycle.

It's my sophomore year, and I'm put into honors classes. The work's harder; I spend lots of afternoons in the library studying. Sometimes instead
of the library, I go to the church. The minister's
daughter is a junior, and I hitch a ride with her.
I'm not sixteen yet, so I only have my learner's per-
mit, but once in a while, when he's feeling good,

Travis lets me his drive his car and comes along for the ride. Those are good days.

The church in the late afternoon is empty and quiet, and daylight hits the rose window high in the back and throws beautiful colored patterns across the stone walls. I walk the long carpeted aisle to the front, light small tea candles, and line them up on the altar rail. And I get on my knees and beg God to make Travis well. *Kyrie eleison. Christe eleison.* . . .

A tear splashes and a tea light sizzles. *Kyrie* . . . *kyrie* . . . *eleison* . . . *eleison.* . . .

I stop abruptly when I hear an unexpected noise behind me. I leap up, turn, and face Cooper standing in the middle of the aisle. "Don't do that!" My voice bounces off the walls.

"Do what?"

"Sneak up on me."

He raises his hands, backs off. "Sorry."

My pounding heart slows. "Wait. I—I didn't mean . . . you just startled me, that's all. Why are you here?"

"To take you home. Your dad's running late, and he called and asked if I could pick you up." Dad usually comes for me after work at either the library or the church.

"I can wait for Dad," I say, feeling self-conscious and wondering how long Cooper's been watching my rituals.

"Not an option. I can wait a little while for you, but I've got to go to work."

It's six o'clock. "Now?"

"New shift at the warehouse. Time-and-a-half pay if I work till midnight."

"I'm ready," I say, looking from the candles I've lit for Travis.

"Do those candles help God see you?"

"Of course not."

"Did God speak to you?"

My face goes hot because he's taunting me. "Please don't make fun of God."

"I'm not."

"Or of me and what I believe."

"I'd never make fun of you, Emily. God, maybe. Never you."

This doesn't reassure me. "Then what's your problem?"

"I don't get how you can keep asking God for something that isn't happening. Is he deaf? Why doesn't he answer?"

Haven't I asked the same question? Why doesn't God answer? I don't want Cooper to see my confusion, so I sling my book bag over my shoulder and head outside into the parking lot to his old tank of a car.

We drive in silence, until Cooper says, "There is no answer, is there? Travis has cancer and your God's pulling the strings and he doesn't have to explain himself, right?"

"Maybe he has another plan," I say in God's defense.

"Then what good is he? To have the power and not use it to help people? God's a fraud."

"Don't say those things!"

"Why not? If he's real, if he's listening, maybe he'll get mad and turn his attention away from Travis and onto me."

His words splash cold water on my anger. When he pulls up in front of my house, he says, "Tell Travis I'll catch him later."

I feel his eyes on me as I leave the car, as his offer to substitute himself for Travis follows me through the front door and into the light.

At the dinner table on Sunday night, Travis asks, "Mom, would you put a DNR on my chart?"

She looks startled. "Where did you hear about a DNR?"

"In the drip unit." That's what he calls chemo. "From a woman with cancer."

"Is this an inquiry or a request?"

"Does it matter?"

"Yes, it matters." Mom puts down her fork. "Do you know what one is?"

"It means they won't revive me if I die."

My stomach seizes. I glance at Dad, then back at Mom and Travis.

"I won't do that," Mom says.

"But I've been thinking about it, and it's what I want."

"Now, you hear me, son. So long as you're alive, we'll never sign a DNR on you."

"But if I won't get better—"

"As long as there's brain activity, people are kept alive. That's medical protocol. We don't kill people who have the hope of recovery."

"What kind of hope have I got? I'm not getting well, and I don't want to be hooked up to a bunch of machines that tie me to a bed for the rest of my life."

"Ventilators help a struggling body breathe. They're wonderful machines."

"And feeding tubes? Are they wonderful too?"

"If it's necessary. A person has to have food and water."

"Why? Why hang on if I'm never going to get better?"

Mom throws down her napkin. "You don't know that. New treatments come along every day."

"But don't I get a say-so?"

"This isn't up for discussion," she insists.

Travis reins himself in. "I don't want to go on life support."

"If you're alive, there's hope. I will never give up hope. And neither should you. Do you hear me?"

They stare each other down.

Dad steps into the fray. "It was only curiosity, Jackie. Wasn't it, Travis?"

Seconds tick away before Travis says, "Sure."

More seconds pass, the only sounds coming from silverware clicking on plates. I've lost my appetite, and I'm pretty sure everyone else has too.

COOPER

The first time Travis tells me what he wants me to help him do, my brain goes numb. He tells me again, and it's like I'm watching those airplanes hit the Twin Towers on TV reruns of 9/11. Like this can't be happening. "What did you say?"

He repeats the words patiently and I know this is no drill. This is real. This is my best friend asking me to help him die.

"That's crazy talk."

"Not crazy." He's holding a pillow against his chest, and every few minutes he buries his face in it, muffling a bad cough. "The cancer's spreading."

This news hits me hard. I want to heave. First the amputation and cancer. Then remission and relapse. Then the spread to his lungs. Now more. I've watched him endure every bit of it. "But all that chemo they gave you. It was supposed to help. Why didn't it help?"

"Luck of the draw, I guess."

"Your mom will find other doctors. She's a bulldog."

He presses the pillow to his face and coughs hard. When the spasm's over, he says, "I don't want to fight anymore. Contest is over. I lose. Help me go out."

I blink, swallow a knot of emotion. "No, I can't."

He catches my arm. "I want a say-so in how this all ends. I want to decide. I don't want the cancer deciding for me. My body. My choice."

"But you might get better—"

"I'm not getting better." He coughs and curses. "Mom's giving me shots and pills round the clock. Oxycontin, vicodin, morphine—none of it stops the pain."

I shake my head. "I can't do it, bro."

"Yes, you can. And I won't ask you to do any-thing that makes people think you helped me. I'll do the deed. I just need your help to do it."

I'm dog tired from all day at school and working a full shift. I've come over late because I know he's awake and alone and in pain. Tonight I wish I hadn't come. "Killing yourself is wrong."

"Why? It's not like I don't have a good reason." He sits up. "I've researched it all on the Web. There are sites that support a person's right to choose to die. Doctors do it for terminal patients every day. It just isn't talked about."

"I'm not your doctor."

"Mom wouldn't let him do it anyway. She's already said as much."

I'm reeling. "Why ask me?"

"Because you're the one person I can count on."

"I don't kill people."

His eyes never leave my face and his voice goes quiet. "If you ran over a dog and it was still alive and suffering, would you help end its suffering?"

"You're not a dog. You're my friend."

"Then be a friend. Help me. If you don't, I'll find someone who will."

I'm cold all over. Really shivering. I know he isn't bluffing. He means it. "It's the pain. If they can control your pain—"

"They can't. I won't die on cancer's timetable." He's getting upset. "I'm going to die. Don't you get that? All I want is to control the timing. Me in the driver's seat. Me going out my way."

My chest feels like it's being crushed with a ten-ton weight. I think about his parents, about Emily, about how they'll feel if he does this. "What about your family?"

"They'll bury me either way. And don't worry, I'll do it in a way so they won't know I did it. I have a plan."

"And what way is that?"

He coughs hard into his pillow, looks over my shoulder, turns pale.

I turn and see Emily standing in the doorway wrapped in a pink bathrobe. "What's going on?" she asks. "It's one-thirty in the morning. What are you two so worked up about?"

Emily

I march into the living room, not one bit self-conscious about being in my robe and pajamas, because the looks on their faces tell me I've interrupted something important.

Travis shakes his head. "Nothing. Guy talk."

Cooper won't look me in the eye. He studies his hands.

"I don't believe you," I say.

"Believe what you want," Travis says. "Why are you up?"

"I heard voices." Not true. I'm having trouble sleeping. I have bad dreams and wake up feeling scared to death.

He coughs into the pillow. "You should be in bed," I say.

"You're not the boss of me."

An attempt at humor—that's what I used to say to him when we were kids and he told me what to do. "Want me to get Mom?" I ask softly when his coughing fit's over.

He shakes his head. I feel helpless and useless. Cooper stands. "I'll take off."

"No, don't leave," Travis says. "Just crash here."

Cooper glances at me, but I don't encourage him. I don't think he should hang around. Travis is all agitated, and Cooper has something to do with it. "Emily's right. You should be in bed, not out here talking to me."

Travis doesn't like the idea. "Why does everyone think they know what's best for me? Don't I get a say-so? I want Coop to stay."

"Later," Cooper says. "I'm fried right now."

Once he's gone, I say to Travis, "I heard you say 'die.' I don't want you to die."

"The whole family would be better off."

"That's not true."

"Yes. It is."

"But—"

"But nothing. Now don't be a snitch and run and tell Mom and Dad."

"I'm not a snitch. But you need to adjust your thinking."

He ignores my lecture, grabs my shoulder. "I want to go to my old room for something. Help me up the stairs."

I lock my arm around his waist and hold him upright while he takes hold of his crutch, and although we go up the stairs together, I feel like there's a wedge between us a mile wide.

I decide to ask Darla if she knows anything about Travis that I don't. I know the two of us will never be best friends, but she's impressed me with her devotion to my brother. I never picked her for the type to stick around, but I'm glad she is.

"What should I know?" she asks me.

"Travis and Cooper are acting sneaky. Cooper drops by practically every night. They act like they've got some big secret, and if I walk into the room, they clam up. This has been going on for over a week. They're up to something."

Her brow knits, but she shakes her head. "Travis hasn't said anything out of the ordinary to me."

I can tell she's clueless, and it irritates me. "What do the two of you talk about?"

"Boring stuff. I tell him about school, cafeteria gossip, who's dating who—anything to keep his mind off of how bad he hurts."

"Well, I'm telling you, something's going on. Something they don't want me to know."

She thinks, nods. "Okay, I'll see what I can find out."

When she turns, the light hits her face in a way that I see a bruise on her cheek. She's covered it with makeup, but I see it faintly spread under her eye.

Jolted, I blurt out, "What happened to you?" and reach toward her face.

Darla pulls away. "Oh nothing. Clumsy me. I walked into a door. Can you believe it?"

I can't, but I let her keep her story. "Well . . . be careful. And—and if Travis tells you something you think I should know—"

"I'll share," she says brightly.

I watch her walk away, and it hits me that Darla Gibson may have secrets too.

Travis

I stand on the towering platform and look down on clear blue water sparkling in eternal sunlight. I already know how it will feel flying downward to meet the water, because I've done this leap hundreds of times. My toes are pointed, balancing my body just on the edge of the concrete, my mind mapping the execution of my perfect dive.

My dive will have a degree of difficulty that's unmatched. I will be the first in diving history to do it in high school competition. The judges look up at me with military attention. Not the usual panel of judges, but instead Cooper, Darla, Emily, Mom, and Dad. I wonder why they're in the jury seats. No matter. I want to be perfect in their eyes and earn perfect scores from each of them.

I stretch my arms over my head, picture the moves in my mind: execute a perfect leap, arms outstretched as if in crucifixion; fold into the pike position; then twist and somersault before I stretch vertical toward the water.

But when I leap something goes wrong. My arms separate from my body, my legs vanish, and I hurtle down toward the concrete-hard water, tumbling out of control, falling, falling. . . .

I wake in a cold sweat. The dream again. Always the same—my body separating, falling apart while people watch. My room is dark, and the last morphine shot Mom gave me has worn off. Dull fire is spreading through my body.

I concentrate on my plan to make the hurting stop forever. It's simple. When the weather warms up, Coop will drive me out to the lake very early one morning. Everyone knows how much I love the lake, so they'll think nothing of our going. We'll rent a canoe at the marina. He'll paddle us out to the deep-water platform, a floating wooden pallet where kids like to hang out in the summer, sunbathing and swimming. We'll be alone. I'll send him to get something I left in the car. He'll return to the shore, make certain he's seen by people, and while he's gone I'll slide off the platform into the water. I'll swim out as far as I can. And when I can no longer lift my arms, when my leg can no longer kick, I'll slip beneath the surface and drown.

That's how I want to end my life, in the water alone, with sky above me, the deep below. And Cooper will be exonerated. An expediter, but a nonparticipant. With only me responsible for the final act. Simple. Just me and the water I love so much. No hospital, no machines, no lingering and waiting for cancer to end my life. My right to die. My life in my control.

And no one will ever know the truth. Except Cooper.

Darla

Emily's right. Travis is keeping something from me. I know because he's my boyfriend. Because I know every inch of him inside and out, and he can't keep a secret from me even if he thinks he can. I know because there's a kind of peace about him I haven't seen in a long time. He's still in horrible pain, but there's something inside him that's different these days. I haven't said anything to him, and he doesn't know I suspect any change, but I know it's there.

We're together every day, alone after his mother leaves and before Emily and his dad come home. I hold him against me when the pain comes. It soothes him to be in my arms. I kiss him, distract him. I love him with all my heart. I hate cancer and his doctors and sometimes even his mother. She's always searching for new treatments that end up building, then dashing, hope.

One afternoon I slip Emily a note to meet me in the school parking lot after the last bell. She's waiting beside my car when I get there. "What's up?" she asks.

"I agree that Travis is holding something back. And I'm sure Cooper's in on it."

"Any ideas?"

"Not yet."

Emily looks disappointed. "Did you ask him?"

"That's not the way it works, Em. I can't pry information out of him. He's got to want to give it up."

She looks baffled, and I realize she's got zero experience when it comes to guys. "Listen, I'll work on Travis and you work on Cooper. He knows what's going on too."

Her face reddens, and she glances in two directions as if we might be overheard. "Cooper! I hardly ever speak to him. Why would he tell me anything?"

"You honestly don't know that he likes you?" This surprises me.

She stutters out, "No way," and blushes bright red. Now I get it. She likes him too but can't admit it.

"He has a soft spot for you, Emily. I thought you knew."

She shakes her head. Denial.

"Trust me. I know these things." I put my hand on her shoulder, look her in the eye. "You're going to have to get him to talk to you. Get him to open up and maybe tell you something that will help us figure out what's going on."

"H-how do I do that?"

"Start by spending time with him."

"Even when he comes over, he hardly talks to me."

"Then talk to him. Ask him to take you to the store or run an errand. It isn't hard to get a guy who's interested in you to spend time with you."

She looks flustered. "I—I don't know. I study most afternoons in the library."

"How do you get home?"

"Dad, usually."

"Well, duh. Ask Cooper to bring you home. I'm betting he'll jump at the chance."

"What if he won't?"

I pat her arm. "He will."

"Is—is that how you got Travis?"

Her chin's tilted, and I see that she's suspicious of me. I realize how calculating I must have sounded to her. "Travis got me," I say. "He got me by caring. That's why I love him. Because he cares and isn't afraid to show it. Isn't that what girls want? Someone who makes us feel special and loved and wanted?"

She doesn't answer me, so I smile and get into my car. "Travis is my one true love," I say out the window. "I'll do anything to make him happy. Got to run. Don't want Travis alone too long."

I drive off, watching Emily trudge toward the school library, and hope she's clever enough to take on Cooper Kulani.

COOPER

Ever since Travis asked me to help him end his life, it's all I think about. I'm on edge, and my temper's out of control. I get into trouble at school. Punched a guy in gym for mouthing off to me. An automatic suspension, but no one rats me out. Smart, because all I want is an excuse to pound on somebody.

I argue with Travis. I tell him I don't want to go through with his plan even though I get his logic. He's shown me stuff from the Internet about death-with-dignity and right-to-die groups like the Final Exit Network and Compassion & Choices. He's shown me the aid-in-dying law that's part of Oregon's state legislation, and examples of eu-thanasia programs in Holland, Switzerland, and

Belgium. "It's civilized," Travis says. "It gives a person a choice over their exit from planet Earth. What's wrong with that?"

"It doesn't feel civilized," I tell him. But he won't stop pushing me to help him. For him it's a head game, a competition, like going after medals in a diving meet: This is what I want. This is how I'm going to get it. "You're playing God," I tell him. I know he believes in that religion stuff.

"You don't believe in God," he tells me.

"Well, Emily does. Would she approve?"

"But Emily isn't going to know, is she? It's just between you and me, bro. My family will never know how it goes down. It'll be an accident. Got that?"

His parents won't even consent to a DNR, something that makes sense to me. It's something I'd want if I were in his place. "What about Darla? You going to tell her?"

His face clouds. "Probably not. She works pretty hard to keep me happy." He shakes his head. "But I hate keeping it from her too."

"Don't you think Darla and Emily will figure it out once it's over?"

"Maybe they will. Maybe they won't. You'd never tell them."

"And don't you think it will wreck them both?"

"I can't think about that." He's pushed back in his dad's recliner; he's just skin and bones, a far cry from the champion athlete I once knew. "I know what I'm asking puts you in a tough place, Coop, but if you just leave me on the platform in the lake, if you take the boat back to shore, if you just play dumb, no one will blame you."

I think, I'll blame me. Does he get how final death is? No turning back. My mouth is sour, and I chase away the taste with a swallow of beer. "You have a time line?"

"Depends on if Darla gets the lead in that play. If she does—well, I wouldn't want to spoil her big moment. I should see her perform."

"Thoughtful of you."

He gives me a cold look. "I know you don't approve, but with or without you, I'm doing this. I'd rather have you with me."

I've had a headache for two weeks, and it's pounding now. "I don't know."

He coughs, finds his breath, and says, "You've got until May. Right before finals week."

"Ironic."

He grins. "So will you help me?"

Emily asks if I can take her home from the library, which surprises me because she pretty much ignores my existence. She's all nervous and jumpy when she asks. I tell her I don't mind, and that's the truth. I don't know why that girl gets to me, but she does and always has. She's nothing like the kind of girl I usually go with.

She doesn't say much when I pick her up in front of the library, but I know something's on her mind. When we get to her house, I ask, "You want a ride tomorrow?"

"Sure. If—if you don't mind."

"I don't mind."

"You still working nights?"

"Six nights a week."

"When do you sleep?"

"First through third periods."

Her smile is pretty. "Don't your teachers notice?"

"Trust me, they'd rather have me asleep."

"Are you going to graduate?"

"Sure. They don't want me hanging around for another year."

"So no college?"

I laugh out loud. "No way. I'm through with school."

"Travis is going to graduate too. More of an honorary degree, Mom says. I wish. . ." Her voice trails off.

"Pick you up tomorrow," I say, not wanting to get into anything else with her, not wanting to make her sadder than she already is.

I drive her home for a week. We don't talk much, but I like her company. I like watching her. She plays with the ends of her hair when she's deep in thought, and she purses her lips when she's thinking over how she wants to say something that's important to her. I drive slowly, wanting our togetherness to last. "I don't mind taking you to church if you want," I tell her. "I'll wait in my car while you do your thing with God."

"No," she says, twirling her hair around a finger. "I don't do that anymore."

Red flag. I hesitate before I ask, "Why?"

"I've done all the begging and praying I can do. God's totally aware of what I want. I've told him hundreds of times."

"But you're not giving up, are you?"

"I think Travis has."

Big red flag. "What do you mean?"

"I think he wants to die."

My heart thuds. Don't go there. "He's in a lot of pain. It can wear a person down."

"I know."

I shift in the driver's seat, search for a way to change the subject. "Look, would you like some dinner? Mo's Pizza Shack is near. I'm thinking a pepperoni, large."

She looks over at me, hesitates. "Let me call Dad and tell him I won't be home for supper."

I can't help myself. I grin like a fool.

Emily

Mo's smells heavenly, all yeasty-rich with baking crust and cheese and tomato sauce. Cooper and I sit in a booth at the back, and he orders colas and a large pizza. Good as it smells, I'm not sure I can eat a bite. There's a candle on our table, and it throws flickering shadows across his face. I think he's gorgeous with his exotic black eyes and brown skin. His hands are huge and rough, but when he shakes hot pepper flakes on the pizza, his hands look gentle. "You mind?" he asks.

"No. I like peppers."

He devours two slices and I nibble on one, wondering how I'm going to get him to talk about Travis, feeling devious when all I want is to feel like a girl on her first date. My heart is hammering hard before I get my courage up and ask, "Do you know what's going on with my brother?"

Cooper stops chewing, drops his half-finished third piece onto his plate. "Why do you ask?"

I'm committed now. "He—he's keeping secrets from me."

"Why shouldn't he have secrets? Any law about not having them?"

"Of course not, but I just have the gut feeling that something serious is going on."

"Talk to him."

"Don't you think I've asked him? He won't tell me. He won't be honest with me."

"And so you thought you'd work on me. Dig it out of me."

The truth hurts, and I squirm. Where is Darla? She should be here. She'd know what to say. "No! I—I mean, I want to know, but that's not why I came here with you. I like being with you." My words are true, but even to my ears they sound insincere.

"Sure you do."

"Please, Cooper . . ."

He studies my face, his dark, dark eyes

unreadable. My heart beats in triple time, and I want . . . I want . . .

"I can't help you." He stands, tosses money on the table for the pizza, and says, "Come on. I'll take you home."

He's almost out the door before I can grab my jacket and catch up with him. At his car, he jerks open the passenger door for me. "Get in."

I hurl myself at him, stand on tiptoe until I'm inches from his body. "You've got to listen to me. This isn't about me or you. I'm going crazy. He's my brother! He's been there all my life." I begin to tremble. "We're a part of each other. If you know something, tell me what it is."

Cooper's face is hard as stone. Did he even hear me? "If you want information about Travis, ask him, not me."

I know what a tough spot I've put him in—tell a secret, betray a friend. It isn't fair, but I had to try. And now, more than ever, I'm frightened for my brother, more scared than in any bad dream I've ever had.

Cooper drives slowly. Night has fallen, and street-lamps make puddles of light on the street and sidewalk. Alexander is a small city, with only a few streets along our downtown. The street he takes is off the main drag. The silence between us is a cold wall. I don't know what to say to make things better. I want information, that's true, but I like being with Cooper, and I don't want him to hate me. In my heart, I like him despite my mother's warnings. If Darla's right about his liking me, I've ruined it.

All of a sudden, Cooper veers the car to the curb and jumps out. "Wait here!"

Alarmed, I shout, "What's wrong?"

He doesn't answer. I watch him run across the street toward two men and a woman. The woman is being shoved between the men, and just before Cooper gets to them, one of the men strikes the woman hard across the face. Then Cooper is in the middle of them, pushing the men aside and yelling, fists flying. He punches and kicks them in a fury until they flee. The woman slumps. Cooper scoops her up in his arms and carries her to the car.

"Get the door, Emily."

I scramble to open it.

He settles her across the backseat and comes

around and gets in the car. He's breathing hard and he's bleeding over his eye. The woman in the back whimpers.

"Who is she?"

He turns the key. "My mother."

I can hardly get my mind around what's just happened. I've never met his mother, and now to meet her like this—

"I have to take her home."

"Sure. Yes. Should she see a doctor?"

"She doesn't need a doctor. She's a drunk, Emily."

"And those two men?"

"Johns."

I know what the word means.

He glances over at me. "You're not going to feel sorry for me, are you?"

In a flash, I understand things about Cooper I never have before, and how Travis has protected him because that's what friends do. I know Cooper's pride is at stake. I regroup quickly. "Of course not. Those men were horrible! Hitting a woman like that. Good thing you came along."

"No biggie."

He pulls into a trailer park and up to a small trailer. I can see its outline in the dark. "Wait here," he says. He takes the woman, his mother, out of the car. With his help, she can stand.

She peers at me. "Are you Coop's girlfriend?" Her words are slurry, but she doesn't seem hurt.

"She's Travis's sister," he tells her.

"Hello," she says, like I'm some long-lost relative. "I always liked your mama. A nice lady. Pitching in to help when Coop was a little guy. He was little once, you know." She pats her son's chest and laughs. She's tiny, with almond-shaped eyes and matted black hair. "Isn't my Coop the best?"

"I'll be right back," Cooper tells me.

I watch him guide her to the trailer and take her inside.

"Yes, he is." There's no one to hear, but I answer her question anyway.

Travis

One quiet afternoon, I tell Darla everything. We're alone in the house, lying together in my bed, skin against skin, April rain sliding down the windows. The soft sound hums, and Darla's arms make me feel safe. I didn't intend to tell her, but the words slip out, a confession from my soul to my soul mate. She doesn't freak out. She listens, smoothing my hair, which is regrowing for the third time since my diagnosis. I feel dampness on my chest. "Don't cry," I tell her. "This is good. It's my choice. It's what I want."

"I knew something was going on inside you. Emily thinks so too. You can't fool girls who love you." She doesn't stop crying. "What about what I want? I want you. For as long as possible."

"My latest labs aren't good, baby. My doc keeps trying, though." My whole chest is sore and raw from where the shunt is inserted for the toxic drugs. "I'm slipping no matter what he does. One day they'll rush me to the hospital and I'll be hooked up to machines that will keep me alive longer than I need to be. I don't want to go out that way." I kiss her forehead. "I'm tired. I hurt all the time."

Now that Darla knows, I feel freer, like a weight's been lifted. "I just want control of my life again. Tell me you understand."

She nods, but the tears don't stop. "When?"

"Soon." I fudge my answer.

"You'll tell me before, won't you? I—I won't have to hear it from your family?"

"I'll tell you."

"Cooper knows, doesn't he?"

"And you. That's all."

"You should tell your sister."

"Fat chance. She'll tell Mom and Dad."

"I'm not so sure. I think she'd understand."

"I can't argue with her. I don't have the energy for it. It's just better that she not know."

Darla raises her head and looks up at me. Her

tears have made tracks down her pretty face. "Will it hurt?"

It takes me a second to figure out what she's asking. "No. It won't hurt. I'll make it simple."

"And you're not scared?"

A hard question, so I take a while to answer. "I was twelve the first time I climbed up on the platform and looked down. Me and my friends were at the city pool, and they were all daring me to go up and jump off. They thought I'd chicken out. I climbed to the top and looked over the edge, and my heart was going a million miles an hour. I wasn't scared. All I wanted to do was fly. And I went off the edge and it was magic. Just me and the air singing past me. I felt like an arrow. I got lucky when I hit the water, because I didn't break any bones. I touched the bottom of the pool and kicked back up feeling like a million bucks. Couldn't hear anything except my own heart beating like a drum.

"Later, Cooper told me the lifeguard was blowing his whistle and screaming because no one under fourteen was supposed to dive from the platform. I was banned from the pool for the rest of the summer, but I knew I'd found my life's purpose. Swim club, the swim team, summers at the lake were for one purpose. I wanted to be the best diver in the state, and someday maybe the best in the country."

I flip Darla's bangs from her forehead, stroke her cheek. "So no, I'm not afraid. Just me and the water. The way I've always wanted it to be."

My parents sit me down and tell me what they think is good news. Mom says, "I'm taking you to Switzerland. You've been admitted into an experimental testing program. It lasts six months and shows a lot of promise for stubborn cases like yours."

She and Dad look at me like I'm supposed to be delirious with joy. "Why?"

"Because it has the potential to turn things around for you," Mom says. "You and I will go together and we'll get an apartment close to the hospital where the program is in place."

I'll be leaving my friends and Darla behind. All things familiar and necessary. "I don't want to live in Switzerland."

"Don't be foolish, son," Dad says. "Your mother's moved heaven and earth to get you accepted. This is a real shot for another remission. Dr. Wolfsen agrees."

What will remission get me? Will it return my lost leg and restore my diving ability?

"Mom, listen to me, I don't want to go."

Dad waves me off. "We totally checked this out, son. This program's had amazing success."

"Like? How much success?"

They glance at one another.

"Fifty percent cure rate," Mom says.

Doctors never use the term "cure." It's "remission," never "cure," because no one's ever cured; you just live waiting and wondering if it's coming back.

"Don't think about percentages," Dad says. "Think about a treatment that works. It helps to keep a positive attitude."

I've been through three protocols of tried-and-true drugs and two protocols of new drugs touted as "revolutionary." For me, nothing has worked.

"Please don't make me go."

Mom looks frustrated. "This is your best hope."

I no longer have hope. "It's in my bones. That's a death sentence." My friend Sally from chemo died last year. Nothing saved her. There was only her long, painful exit from life.

"Don't think that way. We're holding it at bay." Mom takes my hand.

"Won't this cost a lot of money?" I know our insurance is about maxed out.

"That's not your concern."

"Where will you get the money?"

They look surprised, like I'm an idiot and am not supposed to think about such things.

Mom opens her mouth, but it's Dad who says, "We have equity in the house and we're getting another mortgage."

"Phil!" Mom interrupts.

"What? He's not old enough to hear this? If he's old enough to ask, we can level with him."

"It's not about the money," Mom says firmly. "It's about survival. Every day you live, every breath you take, is worth any price we pay. Every day could bring a scientific breakthrough or a new wonder drug. We love you, Travis. We want you with us!"

"Then let me die and have me stuffed."

Mom goes ballistic. "That's not one bit funny, mister!"

I can't tell her I've already made my exit plans. I'm through hanging around dying cell by painful cell. "When are we supposed to go to Switzerland?"

"In June. We can keep you stable until we leave."

May is mine, then. "All right," I say with a sense of relief. "That'll be good timing."

Darla

Funny how priorities change. Two days ago I was totally focused on getting the lead in the school play. It was all I could think about. Then on a rainy afternoon Travis tells me what he's planning, and now I can't think about anything else.

My love is choosing to die. It will be simple, he tells me. As simple as allowing himself to drown in the lake.

I sob and beg him not to do this thing.

All he tells me is "Can't you see it's better this way?"

"Better for who? Not me. I don't want you to die."

He wipes my cheeks. "Living isn't an option anymore. Not this way. If I could have beaten this thing—" His voice cracks and I hug him tight. He tells me, "This is how I win, baby. This is me taking control. Carpe diem."

I can't get my head around this decision he's made. I text him that night, asking him to reconsider. I come back the next day and try again to talk him out of it. He won't budge. I tell him it isn't fair to ask me to keep this terrible secret. When I tell him this, he looks alarmed. "You have to act normal, like nothing's wrong."

"How can I do that? I feel like I'm going to break down and cry every minute."

He takes my shoulders and pulls me close. "You just have to, Darla. Don't betray me."

I go for tryouts in our auditorium with about fifty other kids—mostly seniors. We still don't know what play Mrs. Paulson's chosen; we just know that we'll read parts today and she'll post roles in two days. I've been thinking about this for weeks. I should feel my competitive spirit rise. Instead I feel as if the world's gone dark. I can't stop thinking about Travis.

Mrs. Paulson walks out onstage and gives a welcome speech. She passes out the play books and says that we'll have thirty minutes to read silently, first the synopsis, then the parts. She'll call us up one by one and assign a reading on the spot. How well we do will determine whether we'll get a role. I would have relished the challenge days ago. Now it hardly matters.

I pick up the booklet in my lap. *Our Town,* by Thornton Wilder. I don't know it.

Mrs. Paulson says, "I've chosen this play because it's a classic, because there are eighteen parts, and because the staging is quite simple. It has no props, no scenery. Everything is left to the audience's imagination and to good, convincing acting. It's set at the turn of the twentieth century.

"Let's get reading, shall we?"

It takes me minutes to read the summary and get the gist of the action. It's set in the small town of Grover's Corners, a town much like ours. A stage manager calls the action and inserts comments and explanations from time to time. As I skim the third act, my heart does a stutter step. The lead character, Emily, has died and has made a request of Death.

I can't try out for this play. I have to get out of here.

"Darla," Mrs. Paulson says, "why don't you start us off?"

Everyone turns to look at me, because I don't move.

"Darla?"

Pretend everything is normal.

I rise, walk to the stage, and stand in front of Mrs. Paulson. "This is an emotional ending." She gives me a page number. "I'll read the stage manager. You read Emily's part. To do this well will require you to dig deep within yourself. Let's go for it."

I scan Emily's lines and feel tears well in my eyes. Emily has asked Death to let her relive one happy day from her past before she goes to her grave. Death has agreed, and she has chosen her tenth birthday. In the scene, she sees her parents still young. I read as Emily watching her younger parents, seeing them as beautiful because they are young.

Mrs. Paulson feeds me another line.

And so we go until I reach Emily's most emotional lines, where she realizes that time goes too fast and that people don't take the time to really see one another. Emily's pain becomes unbearable, so difficult that she asks to be taken back "up the hill—to my grave." As she leaves, she cries: "Oh, Earth, you're too wonderful for anybody to realize you. Do any human beings ever realize life while they live it?—every, every minute?"

By now tears are pouring down my face. No one makes a sound. They watch me stand and cry. Suddenly I toss the play booklet to the floor and run backstage where it's quiet. I can't stop sobbing. In seconds, Mrs. Paulson is at my side. "Darla! You've hit a nerve. I can see how you've connected to this role." She touches my shoulder.

I twist away from her and fight hard for composure. Pretend everything is normal. I am an actress.

I brace myself. I force the tears to stop. I replace agony with control. I brush my face, turn, and smile as sweetly as I know how. "Nothing's wrong, Mrs. Paulson. It's called acting. How did I do?"

My performance is the talk of the school, and two days later the parts are posted and I've locked down the part of Emily. When I tell Travis, he gives me a grin and a thumbs-up. "I knew you could do it."

"It doesn't matter," I tell him. "I'm not taking the part."

"What? But you want it."

"I wanted it. I want to be with you more."

"But you shouldn't—"

I gently put my fingers across his lips. "Yes, I should. Great actresses can pick and choose their roles, you know."

I see love in his eyes. "Besides," I say brightly, "the lead character's name is Emily. And I ask you, do you really want two Emilys in your life?"

His laugh warms my heart.

Emily

Okay, it's official. Everybody knows what's going on with Travis except me. Cooper ignores me and Darla won't talk to me. Any direct questions are met with "Nothing's new" or "Ask Travis."

Travis is a sphinx. We don't talk about anything important. He tells me that Mom and Dad are getting on his nerves, and that he hurts, and that he can't concentrate to keep up class work, but nothing about what he's thinking. And that's what I want to know about.

I take matters into my own hands. I raid his computer. I pull down the history of sites he's visited in the past weeks. And my blood runs cold.

I set my alarm for early in the morning

because I want to talk to him before anyone else is up. I just hope it's a night that Cooper isn't crashing on our sofa. I find Travis downstairs, alone, watching a DVD movie, so I know he's been up most of the night, because that's what he does when he's in pain and can't sleep.

"Em. Why are you down here?" He hits the Pause button, and the screen freezes on a car beginning to explode.

I drop a stack of printouts on the coffee table in front of him. "I know you've visited suicide and euthanasia sites online."

"You raided my computer?"

"I followed your footprints."

He glances through the stack, shoves it aside. "Okay. So what?"

"So is that what you're thinking? You want to kill yourself? And Cooper and Darla know, but not me. I'm your sister and you didn't tell me?"

"I didn't want to have this talk with you. And I never want Mom and Dad to know."

"And Mom's making all these plans to get you well—"

"I'm not getting well, Em. Mom's got blinders on. She's obsessed."

"Obsessed? She wants you to live."

His expression twists with pain and he goes pale. After a minute he says, "I just wish my family could crawl inside my skin for a day. I wish you all could feel how I feel. I'll bet none of you could stand it for even twenty-four hours."

I'm sure he's right about that. "Just because you're in pain—"

"I'm a burden to everyone."

He's said this before to me. "You're not a burden, Travis."

"I'm a burden to me." He reaches for my hand. "I wish I could live, Em. Look at my labs, at the numbers. There's no hope of my beating this. And for the record, killing yourself isn't illegal."

I think about all the prayers I've said, all the petitions I've made to God on my brother's behalf. "You don't think it's immoral? Or don't you believe in God anymore?"

"Don't," he says forcefully. "I believe in God, and I'm guessing he'll forgive me. We'll deal with each other when we meet."

"And you're not afraid?"

"Only of being hooked to machines and forced to live when I don't want to. I want to choose my time to die. Everybody dies; that's a fact. Sometimes it blindsides people. Sometimes people get a glimpse of the big picture and decide to cheat. All I've got is timing. It's my trump card."

"Travis, please—"

He ignores me. "Now that you know, don't rat me out, Em. Promise me."

He's asked me this before too. But now the stakes are higher. It's not a matter of being a tattle-tale or a snitch. It's life and death. I want to argue with him. I want to clear out his mind and help him see that what he wants to do is wrong. Instead I don't argue. He's in pain, and nothing I say will get through.

I sit beside him on the sofa, curl into his side, and hold him. Travis turns toward the TV and pushes the Play button, and the car, still mid-explosion, blows into a million fiery smithereens.

I pick a night when the moon is dark. When everyone's asleep, I sneak out of the house and into Travis's car. I hold my breath and start the engine. I drive to the trailer park where Cooper lives, my heart hammering, raw nerves mixing with fear. I find Cooper's trailer, park, and wait. It's almost one a.m. before he drives in. He sees me, comes quickly to the car.

"Travis?"

I hear panic in his voice. "He's all right," I say.

"Why are you here?"

"Because I want to talk to you."

He gets in the car. My heart is pounding so hard I think it might shoot out of my chest.

"I know what's going on," I say. "I know what Travis is planning to do. I visited the sites on the Internet about suicide."

Darkness shrouds Cooper on his side of the car. I can just make out the shape of his body. He says, "Okay, so now you know. Does it help knowing?"

I won't be distracted by his question. I stick to what I've come to say. "I got focused on the suicide part. It's taken me a few days to figure out that the sites were about euthanasia too. Travis can't do this by himself. He's too sick. He'll need help."

He's quiet, and it feels like all the air's gone out of the night. I can hardly catch my breath.

"And you want to know if I'll help him."

Direct. To the point. So like Cooper.

"I haven't said I will yet," he tells me.

"But will you?" I want to hate Cooper. I want

to hit him and never stop. I sit like a statue, unable to move. "Do you think he's right? Do you think he should have a choice?"

"Don't you?"

"I think people should do everything they can to stay alive."

"And Travis hasn't? Look what he's gone through. Look how hard he's fought. And now your mom wants to drag him off to Switzerland."

"It might be the place that saves him."

"And it might mean he'll die a thousand miles from where he wants to be. How can we live with that?"

"But you said you haven't agreed yet. You can stop him." I can't let this go. If I can't change Travis's mind, maybe I can change Cooper's.

"I don't like his plan either. I tried to talk him out of it more than once."

"Try again."

He opens the car door. "Go home, Emily."

"But—"

He slams the car door behind him, and I watch him walk away into the night.

Darla

Emily's waiting for me by my car when school's out Monday afternoon. I'm nervous, because Emily doesn't usually seek me out. The last time, the only time, was when she wanted me to help her uncover Travis's plans. Now that I know his plans, I don't want to face her.

"Let's go get coffee," she says.

My tummy flips. "But I'm supposed to be with Travis."

"Mom's going in late to work. I told her you had to help with the school play."

"But I'm not in the play."

"A white lie, so sue me."

There's no getting out of going with her. We drive to a coffee shop in a strip mall near the school. We order two syrupy flavored coffee drinks, find a small table by the window, and sit across from each other. Not enemies, but not friends either.

"I know what Travis is planning to do." She wastes no time getting to the point.

"He told me you knew."

"And you aren't going to stop him? You're going to let him?"

"How can I stop him?" I lean closer. "I don't want him to. I've asked him, begged him not to. It hasn't made a difference."

"So you agree with this idea?" Her eyes are blazing.

"I agree that he has the right to decide what he wants to do with his life. People have choices, you know—about good and bad things to do." I think of my mother. "I don't agree with a lot of choices people make, but it's still their choice."

"Even when the choice hurts other people?"

"If the other people don't know, how can they be hurt?" I get that "other people" to Emily are her parents.

"Don't you believe in right and wrong?"

"If I blew up this coffee shop, that would be

wrong because I'm hurting people who don't deserve it. But what Travis wants to do won't harm anyone who doesn't know the truth. That's our part—to keep others from finding out."

"But we know. And Cooper's going to help him. That's illegal."

I shrug, take a sip of the sickly sweet drink. "So is underage drinking and smoking weed. But people do it anyway." I know Emily's kind of religious, but she's asked for my honest opinion, and I'm giving it to her. "I don't want to lose Travis," I tell her. "If I could change things, I would. We all would."

Tears fill her eyes, and she slumps. "It's just because of the pain. He's not thinking clearly. If they could fix his pain . . ."

My own eyes fill up. "Taking away pain won't change things for him. He wants to call the shots for his life. And right now, all I want is to love him. So that's what I'm doing."

She stares out the window for so long that I'm wondering if she's checked out. Finally I ask, "Will you tell? Or will you let him do what he wants?"

COOPER

Travis wants to go to the district diving competition. I think he's nuts, but I agree to take him. His mom shoots him up with morphine before we leave the house.

"A legal high," he says. "It's not what it's cracked up to be."

The bleachers are crowded on the spectator side of the pool, and flags in school colors are flapping in the breeze. I'm pushing him in a wheelchair, and he's covered up because chemo and sunlight don't mix. He hasn't worn his prosthesis in months, so he hangs a blanket across his lap to hide his empty pants leg. When we go onto the pool deck, the whole team erupts with hoots and hollers.

"Good to have you with us," Coach Davis says, patting Travis's shoulder. He doesn't say the same thing to me.

"I wish it were me up there," Travis says, looking at the springboard.

Coach nods. "We all do."

Once the competition starts, Travis studies every dive the way a starving man stares at food. Lenny's the leader, the one to beat. Travis would be the one if he were up there. If only there were some kind of magic that could turn back time and erase what's happened to him. I clear my throat. The knot that's there never seems to go away.

"How are you doing?" I ask him midway through the meet. Fine beads of sweat cover his face, but not from the heat. I'm guessing he's feeling pretty bad.

"Hanging in."

I slip him a pain pill.

Travis's presence inspires our team. They're always good, but today they're brilliant. The judges reward them with high scores and the district title. We stay through the medal ceremony, during which Lenny's given a gold medal for best individual performance. As the crowd breaks up and the team heads for the locker room, Lenny comes over. He holds out his hand and Travis shakes it. "Glad to see you, man. Thanks for coming."

"Didn't want to miss it."

Travis asks to see the medal and Lenny hands it over. "You want it?" Lenny asks.

"I didn't earn it."

"You would have. You're better than me."

Travis grins. "I know." He hands the medal back. "Where you going in the fall?"

"University of Miami."

"Great aquatics program. Make us proud."

"That's my goal."

We watch Lenny walk away, his wet skin glistening in the sunlight. Travis stares into the deep end of the blue pool water. "I'm ready to leave," he says.

And I know he's talking about more than the ride home.

I'm at his place on Saturday night, and it's late. I'm eating popcorn and drinking a beer. Travis is in the recliner sipping cola because it helps with nausea. He tells me that Darla knows everything, and I'm thinking Darla will be his backup plan, because the girl will do anything for him. He adds, "Emily knows too. She figured it out."

I tell him about her coming to see me and ask, "Is your secret safe?"

"So far she's kept it to herself."

"I don't think she'll say anything." I'm not as confident as I sound.

"She told you not to help me, didn't she?"

I stop midswallow.

"Did she persuade you?"

My hand tightens on the bottle. "I didn't commit either way."

"Are you thinking she'll hate you if you help? Maybe not right away, but eventually?"

He's seen inside me, like he usually does, and hit the mark. Of course she'll hate me. "Why should it matter?"

"Because you love her."

I feel my face get hot. "How long have you known?"

"For years. You've never hid it real well."

"I never followed through on it either."

"Maybe you should have."

"It wouldn't work out."

"If you help me, probably not," he says. "She'll

never look at you the same way again. I'm sorry for putting you in this spot."

I make up my mind in an instant. "No use holding out for something I can't have. I'll take you to the lake," I tell him. "You pick the day."

Emily

I'm alone in my room. I spend a lot of time alone these days. Foreknowledge is a burden, a weight I can hardly bear. Maybe that's why God keeps the future hidden from us. If I knew I would have a terrible accident, would I live my life trying to avoid it? Would I lock myself inside a room being safe? Or would I go outside and live day to day?

Do I blow the whistle on Travis's plans? What would Mom and Dad do—check him into a psych ward? Lock him up? Telling will add days to a life Travis no longer wants to live. Not telling will take him away so much sooner.

I stare at the table beside my bed. There's a lamp. My cell. My alarm clock. A glass of melted ice and cola, making water rings on the wood. These are real and solid. I can touch them, understand them. I see my Bible. It's a pointing finger into my heart. *Kyrie eleison.* Maybe that's all I have, all Travis has—God's mercy.

He's my brother. I want to be with him, no matter what.

I pick up the Bible and walk it to my closet, open the door and drag my desk chair over. I climb on the chair, stand on my tiptoes, and reach for the farthest, darkest corner. I place my Bible on the shelf, as far out of my sight and reach as possible.

Travis

"How?" Emily comes into my room and sits in the chair beside my bed.

I'm hooked up to a home dialysis unit, so I can't get away from her. Her question is obvious. No use pretending that I don't know what she's asking. It's been days since she discovered my plan, and she walks around like a ghost, hardly speaking, making Mom and Dad wonder what's wrong with her. She hasn't given me away, and she hasn't tried to talk me out of it again. A surprise.

"The lake," I say. "I want the water to do the job." She looks horrified, so I keep explaining, wanting to settle her down. "I've thought it out. Mom keeps my pain pills under lock and key. So no 'accidental' OD. I told Cooper and Darla how

I can do it with insulin. Did you know insulin's untraceable in the bloodstream? I showed them my Web research, how it's been done that way before. But then I realized someone would have to buy the insulin for me, and Mom and Dad might figure it out since no one's a diabetic, and my helper would be outed. And prosecuted. And that's not what I want to have happen."

"Travis, listen to yourself. You sound like you're picking something off a menu! Pills, insulin, drowning—"

I interrupt her. "I want a way that won't scream 'suicide.' I'm trying to protect my family. If you hadn't been so dog determined, you wouldn't have to know any of this."

She looks away, stares into space. The sound of the dialysis machine doing its job fills the silence. Finally she turns to me. "When?"

"To be determined."

"When?"

My answer doesn't deter her. "It has to be warm enough," I explain. "So that going to the lake will make sense. No room for questions from Mom and Dad."

"Just you and Cooper."

"Yes."

Silence.

"It would be better if we all went together."

Her words stun me. Did she really say that? "All of us?"

"Darla, me, Cooper . . . like old times. It'll be more believable for Mom and Dad that way."

Suddenly I'm not sure. Maybe this is a trick. "Are you planning to have them jump out of the bushes and throw a net over me?"

"I know you're going to do what you want to do even if they lock you in an empty room. I can't stop you."

True.

She looks at her folded hands. A tear trickles down her cheek, and I almost fall apart.

"Em, you don't have to be there."

"Yes, I do. I'm family. Someone from your family should be with you. You need to know that I love you. No matter what."

I'm reminded of when she was a little girl and I was confined to my room for doing something I shouldn't have done. I was in solitary—no TV, no video games. I was allowed out only to go to the bathroom and to go downstairs for meals. Emily sat in a chair outside my door for two days. Mom tried to get her to leave, told her that she wasn't being punished, that she was a good girl. Emily just looked up at her and said, "That's okay. I'll wait here." And she did. She slid a drawing in bright red crayon under my door, of an eye and a heart and the letter "U" . . . "I love you."

Looking at her now, I know I want her to be there. I want Darla to be there too. I want to see them on the shore before I dive off the platform. I want them on the shore when Cooper returns. He'll need them.

"Thanks, Em," I say, and reach out my hand.

She takes it, and we sit together like that for a very long time.

COOPER

I want to knock holes in walls with my bare fists.

Travis had a seizure, a stroke that paralyzed him on one side, and now he's trapped in ICU, stuck with all the medical crap he was trying to avoid. Tubes seem to be coming out of every part of his body, and machines surround his bed like birds of prey. He's alive—a machine breathes for him, another monitors his heart; another cleans his kidneys. He still has brain activity. I know that's true because his eyes follow me in the room if he's awake.

This isn't what he wanted. All we needed was a few more days and he could have avoided this. We were going to the lake early on Saturday morning—all of us. And Travis would have slipped into the water from the platform and his life would have ended the way he wanted. His death would have been an accident.

School's over for the year, and by some miracle, I graduated. Mom cleaned herself up to go to the ceremony, but I barely remember it. Travis was given a diploma and a standing ovation, but he wasn't there to receive either. I spend all my free time at the hospital with Darla and Emily in the ICU waiting area. Days drag by. Travis is allowed visitors for ten minutes once an hour. The rules say only family is admitted, but his mother has cleared the way for Darla and me to visit him twice a day each. I have to force myself to go into his cubicle, because I can't stand seeing him the way he is. But I can't stand not seeing him either.

He turns eighteen while in ICU. Emily has words with her mother in the waiting area in front of me and Darla. "He wanted a DNR."

"No DNR," her mother says. "That's final."

Of course he can't even sign his name on the paperwork, so his parents still rule his life.

Emily keeps us updated. "They're inserting a feeding tube," she tells us. "For better nutrition. I told Mom he'd hate it, but she won't listen to me.

It seems that the cancer is in check for a while too. And his heart's still strong."

Any other time this would be good news.

Emily adds, "They're moving him into a private room, so we'll be able to visit him more often."

"Will he still be on all those machines?" Darla asks.

"Yes, but we can talk to him. Doctors say that hearing is really good for patients like Travis. We can read to him too."

Her face is so childlike and trusting that I have to look away.

"We're in this together, aren't we?" she asks.

"Like how?" I ask.

"Working to make things better for him. Just like we've done before." She holds out her fist.

I consider our circle—bound by our loyalty to Travis, willing to help him die, now caught in the web of medical science keeping him alive. It's a roller-coaster ride of hoping he'll beat all odds and fear that he won't. Of knowing what we were willing to do for him, and now what we can't do at all.

"I'm in," Darla says, tapping Emily's fist.

They look to me. I hold out my fist and we seal our pact again.

One afternoon, Darla comes to the cafeteria looking for Emily and me. Her skin is ashen.

"What's wrong?" I ask.

"I think he's in pain," she says. "His body keeps jerking and they tied down his arms so he won't pull out any of the tubes."

My best friend, tied to a bed.

"What's the worst that can happen?" I ask Emily.

Days later, Emily tells us. "His doctors want to cut off his other leg to help his circulation. And they want to sew his eyelids shut because he can't blink on his own and his corneas are drying out."

His doctors never get to follow through with their plans, though, because the next night, the twenty-fifth of June, Travis's heart stops beating and he can't be revived.

Emily

*M*y brother dies in the early morning, when the world is at its darkest, when no one's around him except IVs, tubes, and machines. Mom is beside herself because she wasn't at Travis's side. Dad tries to console her. "Jackie, we couldn't be there twenty-four seven and still function. We did all we could do."

I cry, but I can't say I'm sorry, because I know how he felt about his life.

We bury Travis in the town's oldest cemetery on a hot June afternoon in a private ceremony. The high school holds a memorial service for him in the football stadium, and half the town shows up. The aquatics team wears black armbands.

Darla comes with her mother and kid sister

but not her father. Cooper shows up with his mother. She looks small and neat in a skirt and blouse, with her black hair pulled back in a bun and fastened with ornamental ivory sticks at her neck. She hugs my mother and father and me. If she remembers me from that night in the spring, she doesn't show it. We all sit together and listen to people say inspiring things about my brother. And we cry.

Days later, Cooper and Darla and I meet at the lake for our own private memorial service. I drive Travis's car. He gave me the keys for my birthday. "Now you won't have to sneak it," he said.

The lake air smells like summer, like coconut sunscreen and Alabama earth and mown grass. Boats zip past far out in the water, their motors sounding like droning bees. I think of other summers when we came, just the four of us, for swimming, and island picnics, and waterskiing. Now we are three.

We hold hands at the shoreline, tell stories of our best memories of my brother, watch kids dive off the floating wooden platform. The ache inside me throbs. I miss my brother. I wish he could have gotten well—it happens for lots of people who get cancer, just not for Travis. When we're through, we stand shoulder to shoulder, awkward and silent, missing the glue of my brother's life that held us together.

I ask, "So what are everyone's plans?"

"The army," Cooper says. "I'm headed to boot camp in a week."

My knees go weak. He's leaving.

He turns to Darla. "How about you?"

"Birmingham," Darla says. "I'm going to live with my sister and her little boy. She had a boyfriend, but he moved out." She motions toward her car. "I'm packed and loaded. No reason to stay here now. I'm going to get a job, maybe help out in a community theater. I've always wanted to be an actress."

Knowing she's leaving for good tugs on my heart. I regret ever thinking she was fluffy like a marshmallow. She stayed with my brother through it all, and I should have tried harder to be her friend. "I'll miss you," I say.

She looks doubtful, but the look passes and she hugs me. "Take care of yourself." She hugs Cooper too, then turns and goes to her car and drives off.

"What about you?" Cooper asks. "What are you doing?"

"I'm going on a mission trip with my youth group. We're building a church in Mexico. In a village that doesn't have one."

He grins. "I guess I shouldn't be surprised . . . although I'll never get how you can believe in someone you can't see or touch."

I look up at Cooper, at the hard planes of his face and his dark eyes. "That's why it's called faith."

He lifts my chin and my heart races. For a second I think he'll bend down and kiss me. Instead he brushes my hair off my shoulder and takes a step back, and the moment is gone. "Have a good life, Emily Morrison."

"Will you write to me?" I ask, not wanting to lose him.

"Maybe."

I watch him walk to his car, and I'm filled with emotions I can't name or number. So many changes to my life. So much I want. So much I long for. He drives away while I stand on the edge of the lake alone, only me and memories and the sun and the sky and the blue, blue water.

My final words on what happened on June 25, 2:55 a.m.

I slip into the hospital wearing scrubs and a lab coat I lifted from a laundry bin days before. I look like I belong on staff, maybe a lab tech. Travis's room is dimly lit, and the only sounds are the hiss of the ventilator and the beep of his heart monitor. The nurses' station isn't far down the hall, so I move quietly.

I stand beside his bed, staring at him, and tie on a surgical mask. He doesn't know I'm here, but if he saw me, he'd know me by my eyes. And he'll know why I'm here.

I reach into the pocket of the lab coat. Once I'd decided I had to do it, I managed to swipe two syringes with insulin. No one saw when I took them. I'd watched so I knew when it was possible, so no nurse would know. It wasn't easy, but I was determined. I have to work fast, because the machines' alarms will sound and nurses will come running once his heart stops. Travis is so sick; he's had a stroke, he's living on borrowed time. No one will question his death.

This is what he wants. He told us. There is no doubt in my mind. I take a deep breath. "Goodbye," I whisper.

Then, before I lose my nerve, I stick one syringe into an IV line inserted in his arm and push the plunger. I follow it with the second, the insurance syringe.

I drop the empties back into the lab coat pocket and ease from the room, hugging to the wall like a shadow. I move quickly toward the side exit door and my escape. I hear the noise of a machine before the inside door clicks shut behind me.

I run down the stairwell, ripping off the lab coat as I go. I wad it up and stuff it under my arm. I leave the hospital and walk briskly into the night.

Travis is free from his tortured body. I have given him what he would have given himself if he could have. No one will ever know what I've done, because his death was expected. No one would ever guess I was the one who did it, and I'll never say a word to the others even though we had a pact to do it together. My silence forever is the only answer.

I know what I did and why I did it. Am I a killer, or a deliverer? I believe I am an Angel of Mercy.

Who's my judge?

Lurlene McDaniel began writing inspirational novels about teenagers facing life-altering situations when her son was diagnosed with juvenile diabetes. "I saw firsthand how chronic illness affects every aspect of a person's life," she has said. "I want kids to know that while people don't get to choose what life gives to them, they do get to choose how they respond."

Lurlene McDaniel's novels are hard-hitting and realistic, but also leave readers with inspiration and hope. Her books have received acclaim from readers, teachers, parents, and reviewers. Her novels *Don't Die, My Love; I'll Be Seeing You;* and *Till Death Do Us Part* have all been national bestsellers.

Lurlene McDaniel lives in Chattanooga, Tennessee.